The Daughter of F
-Written E
Shameek A. S

D1527849

Copyright © 2021 by True Glory Publications
Published by True Glory Publications
Join my Mailing List by texting
shameekspeight to
844-484-0922

Facebook: Shameek Speight

Cover Design: Tina Louise
Editor: Venitia Crawford-Fergus

retrieval system, without the written permission
from the publisher and writer. Because of the dynamic nature of the Internet and Web addresses or links contained in this book may have changed since publication and may no longer
be valid. The views expressed in this work are
solely those of the author and do not necessarily
reflect the views of the publisher, and the publisher hereby disclaims any responsibility for
them.

Table of Contents

Chapter 1

Alarms and red lights were going off all through the building, a few henchmen were still fighting soldiers, but everyone was trying to escape, running for their lives, even the hyenas that was left was looking for a way out as the building continued to collapse.

Jainice had Minglee, Meashell and Egypt by her side and Raven flying above her. As they ran to the jungle room. The second she seen J-Money laying outside the doorway, made Jainice want to scream but she held it in. She ran over to him and was shocked to see he was still breathing but barely alive. "Oh God no!" Jainice screamed when she looked at Faith, legs bust open as if someone try to rape her, bullet holes in her chest and shoulders, Jainice got close and could see roaches in the womb of Faith stomach, just running around , looking like a nest or a project home where roaches run the walls all day. She moved closer and could hear Faith breathing, it was shallow but she was still fighting to stay alive. "Help me with her, we can get her out of here then find a doctor." Jainice said.

Minglee looked at her as if she was dumb, are you crazy or slow. "Fuck that bitch." Minglee said as she ran over to Faith and kicked her in the ribs.

"No," Jainice said pushing Minglee feet away.

"You lost your mind that bitch kidnapped us, we're free now, let her die and let's go!" Meashell said.

"What about Tammy, we don't know where she is," Jainice said.

"Fuck Tammy! We don't know if she's alive, right now we alive and that won't last for long if this building come down over our heads or if we run into more of those soldiers." Minglee said.

"I'm not leaving her, she wouldn't leave us just like that, she even came and got us out that damn desert room." Jainice said.

"Man fuck that bitch," Minglee said and tried to kick Faith again.

Jainice jumped up and punched her in the mouth, "Don't kick her when she down, don't kick any one when they down," Jainice said.

"Man fuck you bitch and fuck her, I hope y'all die together." Minglee said.

"Bitch that's how you really feel, I knew you for years, you're like my sister." Jainice replied.

"Naw, dead that sister shit, fuck you and TGP that's how I feel," Minglee said.

"You too Meashell?"

Meashell kicked Faith in the head "Fuck that bitch and you, you got Stockholm syndrome hoe. Fuck y'all," Meashell said then spin kicked Jainice in the chest , she trip over Faith body and fell to the ground and Minglee and Meashell started to kick her in the face and ribs.

"Stupid bitch, we free" Minglee shouted. Jainice grabbed her leg and punched her in the pussy then stomach. "Let go of me!" Minglee shouted. "I won't die here with you or that bitch," Minglee said but Jainice wouldn't let go of her leg.

Meashell kicked Faith in the head twice Jainice let go of Minglee leg and popped up, Meashell spit on Faith and took off running with Minglee behind her. "Fucking hoe," Jainice said ready to chase them but felt Faith hand grab her leg.

"No, don't go," Faith said weakly. Jainice looked down, "We got to get out of here." Jainice said as she looked at the wheel chair.

"Did you bring the black case under my bed?" Faith asked.

"Yea it's right here," Jainice replied.

"Open it, grab the green syringe and stick me with it, and grab the orange one inject yourself and J-Money." Faith was barely able to say.

"How is this going help, how?" the building coming down Jainice said but Faith was no longer talking. Jainice popped open the case to see hatchets and an axe, twin guns, a bodysuit and two syringes. She grabbed the green one and jammed the needle in Faith's neck, pushing the liquid into her system, then she rolled her sleeves up and injected herself with the orange one, then ran over to J-Money, "I'm sorry about this, it's not sanitary J-Money," Jainice said then jammed the needle in his neck and pushed the liquid in.

People could be heard screaming as more of the building collapsed, Jainice looked at a huge piece of the ceiling fall blocking the exit to the room and knew she wasn't escaping. She crawled over to Faith and held her head in her lap and started to cry knowing she was about to die. Faith opened her eyes with the little strength she had and touched Jainice face.

"My father said I can trust you, he was right. Do you trust me?" Faith asked.

Jainice continued to cry. "Yes I trust you," she said as the rest of the building collapsed and the ceiling came down crushing her and Faith and J-Money alive.

Chapter 2

"There's no point she's dead, there all dead. It's been a month!" Cricket shouted at Lefty, as him and twenty henchmen and bulldozers pulled chunks of rocks out from the ground from the collapsed building.

"Why you're so fast to give up?" Lefty asked while watching the men work.

"Because man, we done pulled out bodies of those military soldiers crushed to death by the building and bodies from our people, and we only made it to the second floor. Faith was on the fourth floor pregnant and weak, I think we should just give up," Cricket said.

And do what? Huh and do what? No one have seen or heard from Black Ice in six weeks!" Lefty replied.

"Listen I love her just like you did, but this is a waste of time. I'm loyal to her, don't question that; I'm saying we need to make plans and take steps on what we're going to do next, and that's if Black Ice don't chop us up and put us in jars for us for letting his only daughter get killed, when we was supposed to protect her. What the fuck we gonna tell him? I went for a truck and you grabbed her mother and while we was outside fighting soldiers the building collapsed killing everyone inside. Shit, we definitely going into a jar, I can see my head now floating in a giant mason jar looking likes a pickle or you know when you go to those low budget bars and see an egg just floating in a jar that's gonna be us my friend." Cricket replied.

"We'll face any repercussions when it's time, the fact of the matter we let her down but we shouldn't have listened to her, we should've put her safety first, that was our job and we failed our job brother. I understand what you're saying, what's next for us, we will go work at another compound but not until we find her body. I'm not leaving her like this, we left her once we not gonna do it again no matter what," Lefty said.

"You're right." Cricket replied.

"We pass the third floor, and about to start removing pieces of the ceiling from the fourth floor now." A henchmen said and Lefty moved closer to the big hole in the ground where the building was.

"I never knew why Black Ice built down," Cricket said.

Lefty looked at him as if to say, really. "Fool because we're in the middle of a forest, trying not to be discovered, kidnapping people, running an international sex trafficking ring. We can't built a building up like a skyscraper, building it down is smart, we had more than enough space and was unseen. What I think was needed is more exits and stronger brick and steel for the future, now we got soldiers with explosives blowing the hell out the building," Lefty said.

"They would've never gotten close if all the henchmen was here, they got us lacking, off guard and without all of our numbers," Cricket said angry.

"Facts, but we can't cry over spilled milk; we'll make them pay for killing Faith." Lefty said.

After three hours of them digging a henchmen shouted "We found something."

Lefty ran to a ladder and climbed down to the fourth floor, knowing he was gonna cry once he seen Faith's squished body . He stepped off the ladder with Cricket behind him. The cautiously walked through the rubble and passed a few henchmen, they walked up to a group of five henchmen moving rocks and collapsed ceiling out of one area. They saw the white gown Faith had on, and her legs first. You can only see her bottom half. They moved the rock over her face to reveal Faith head, which was resting in Jainice lap, both women were crushed, every bone in there body broken.

Lefty tried to fight back the tears. Roaches scattered around their bodies and could see bite Marks on Faith and Jainice bodies. The roaches ran up under another rock. Lefty try to hold back his tears and was happy he had his mask on. "Get their bodies out of this place," Lefty said with a shattered voice as if he was going bust out crying any second.

"What the fuck! What the hell!" one of the henchmen yelled, then another as Faith's body began to reshape and so did Jainice, then Faith's chest started to move up and down.

"No this can't be right, it must be roaches inside them, making them move," Cricket said.

"No! No it's not. I've seen this before with Black Ice and you remember that fat bitch Red Velvet?" Lefty said.

"Yea, the one Faith chopped her legs off and pinned to the wall for about two weeks." Cricket replied.

"Right," Lefty said while smiling.

"Ughh!" Faith coughed up dust, dirt, and some roaches while gasping for air. "My baby! My baby!" she screamed while crying.

The henchmen looked at her in amazement. Then Jainice started coughing up dirt and roaches and moved very slow and raised her arm and pointed.

"What she pointing to?" Cricket said.

"Get your asses over there and move those rocks over there!" Lefty shouted, they rushed to the spot Jainice had pointed to and quickly started throwing rocks to the side to see a large man's body. Once the rocks was off him, he started to cough. "Get blankets," Lefty said as Faith continued to scream and cry.

"They took my baby! They took my baby ahhhhhh!" Jainice continued to hold her as Cricket placed a blanket on both of them and hugged them and Lefty bent down and hugged Faith.

"We will get them Mistress. We will get them." Lefty said while crying. Seeing her in pain broke everyone's heart that could hear her cries and screams.

"That bitch and her husband took my baby! My baby!"

14

Faith soaked in the tub hoping it would ease her mind, but knowing deep down nothing would because a part of her had been taken, maybe forever. She looked down at her stomach, even though it had healed it still looked like a c-section scar. She stepped out the tub and Jainice was there waiting with a towel and wrap it around her. "You don't have to baby me or cater to my every need; Jainice you're not a slave but my friend," Faith said.

"I know, but I also know how much you're hurting and know you'd do it for me. I'm never leaving your side and you know that." Jainice replied.

"Why? Why didn't you leave me like Minglee and Meashell, why? Why are you still here? I told you that you're free," Faith said while sitting down on the edge of the bed and started applying lotion to her legs.

Jainice pulled out a blunt and led it, her hair was in a ponytail, she was dark brown-skin complexion and 5'6 tall. You could tell she was African from her facial features, she was beautiful with nice lips and not slim or thick but in between. Jainice flopped down in a grey chair that was in the room and pulled on the blunt. "You really asking me this after what we just been through?" Jainice said talking with smoke in her mouth.

"I'm sorry, but my man betrayed me and ran off with my money, the woman I loved and like at as a mother figure cut me open and took my child and shot me five times; I got trust issues," Faith said shaking her head.

"I'm not gonna say, I told you so to kick you when you're down, but everyone kept saying something was funny with Jason and that old lady just gave me the creeps. I told you that, but who am I to judge you, two women I knew my whole life, pretty much said fuck me and gave me their asses to kiss. I'm not leaving because my eyes are open to another world and they can never be closed again. Acting like monsters and killers aren't real, I think people don't want to see, their mind can't handle it. Next bitch, I showed you I'm with you to the end, when that building was coming down on us. I didn't leave you, I honestly thought that was the end. I'm gonna die right here with you, not let you die alone, I didn't think for a second I'd be sitting here alive when I made that decision, so don't question my loyalty ever. I pretty much died for you and with you." Jainice said.

Faith stood up and walked over to her and hugged her. "I know, but they broke me," Faith said while crying.

"Don't you cry, you're the daughter of Black Ice, the fucking devil himself, a real life serial killer. They broke you, what should you do?" Jainice said breaking their embrace and passed Faith the blunt.

"You always talk all deep and shit when you get high," Faith said inhaling and wiping her tears away. "I'm going to break them, I'm going make them feel my pain," Faith said.

"That's my bitch! Jainice said.

"You know you'd never talk to me like that before until we died together," Faith said.

"Shit I'm not scared of dying no more, been there. I'm not about to be running around like, "Yes Mistress," you're still my boss but now you're my friend, speaking of not dying shit, how does this work?" Jainice said as Faith passed her the blunt then she pressed the blunt fire to the back of her hand and it burnt her skin dark black like it had been on the grill.

"From what my father told me it's a formula or virus made by the Asians, and he got it from a group of women assassins called the Teflon Divas.

You'll still feel pain, it will make you faster and physically stronger and you can heal. The one that's in me, I'll heal faster; your healing kicks in after ten minutes or so and the formula not as strong as the one in me or my father or the Divas and you can still die. We die and think our bodies was crushed, so it didn't heal until the pressure was off of us, and when I was fighting that bitch Red my father said if I chop off her head she was good as dead, that all I know about it, shit I never wanted to use it. He pretty much ordered me to take, I thought if I start using the things he gave me I'll be more like him, that he was wrong about people. But it turned out he was right and if my stupid ass would've been took the formula. That old bitch couldn't poison me to make me weak," Faith said getting sad and depressed again.

"We can't talk about what we could have done, but we can talk about what we will do," Jainice said relighting the blunt and watching the back of her hand slowly heal. This shit cool as fuck. I feel like Wolverine bitch," Jainice said laughing and passing the blunt to Faith.

"Wolverine? Faith asked confused.

"Yea, while we kill people, you need to start watching tv and movies. That shit helps in life, you'll be able to relate to some shit or see certain things coming ahead of time because you'll be like

I seen this shit happen before on this show or movie, trust me," Jainice said.

"Whatever," Faith said as a knock was at the door. "Come in," Faith said.

"Mistress and Jainice," Lefty said. He had his mask off, and Faith was happy about it, because she knew Lefty was her right hand man and one of the people she could count on and his facial expression lit up with joy when he seen her, something his mask would hide. "I have good news and bad," Lefty said as he passed Faith an Apple laptop.

"What's the bad news?" Faith asked.

"We haven't heard from your father, none of the other compounds, safe house henchmen or doctors have seen him, but Black Ice network reached far in different countries. The henchmen in Houston Texas are… Hmm what the word I'm looking for, are nervous, but want to see you. They never met you and know we're here, but I know you're not ready to go to another base that's underground, I can fully understand. I hate going there myself after what we just been through but they need to see your face, with your father gone, things are still running the same but you gonna have to pop up. Next, I still got no word on Antonio and Sabrina, we're trying to track down the army mercenary team they hired. Once we do that, we can locate them and your baby. Next, there's no word on the streets or sight of Minglee and Meashell. They was with us for two years so they know how to move and hide but they'll get comfortable and mess up. Until then, we have the technical team using facial recognition software. Let's just hope they don't change the face before we find them," Lefty said.

"Naw they're both to conceded for that, if anything they'll try to leave the United States and head to Africa to hide. Minglee's family from Ganja and Meashell got people in Nigeria, with the money they made with you and they're new skills they'll be like queens there," Jainice said.

"I didn't know y'all all was African," Faith said.

"You never ask," Jainice replied.

"Okay fuck all the bad news, what's the good news? Faith asked.

"We found Jason," Lefty said.

The room went silent. Faith opened the laptop and could see pictures and videos of Jason caught by companies surveillance camera and street cameras. "How long he's been there? Do he know we found him?" Faith asked as her anger grew.

"We have a team watching him now, but I thought you'd want to handle this yourself, and oddly I don't think he's even watching over his back. He's living like he has no concern in the world." Lefty replied.

"That's because he thinks I'm dead. He's the one that sold out our location to Antonio and his private army, he has no ideas we made it out alive." Faith said.

"It will take us a two hour flight from Houston to get there." Lefty said.

Jason sat at the poker table and studied the other five players before he threw down his cards, full house!" he shouted.

"Damn!" everyone said at the table as the dealer pushed over $300,00 in casino chips.

He quickly grabbed them up as one of the casino managers came over, "Hey do you want a complementary room in the hotel it's on the house?" he said.

"No thank you, I'm getting good at this gambling thing and learn it's best to take the money and run, and try a different casino. If I stay in one spot too long that's how y'all get me. I'm good," Jason said as he walked to the slot machine to tip a young Spanish man on the shoulder that had on clothes that was way too small for him.

"Francis, Let go!" Jason said.

"Not now daddy, let me play two more games, I'm about to hit it big, I just know it." Francis replied.

"You already hit it big when you got me, now let's go or I'm leaving without you," Jason said as someone tried to rush pass him.

A big baldhead Caucasian man dressed in a black suit yelled "Stop that guy!"

"Walk around," he said in a deep voice.

Jason turned around and faced the 6'4 stocky man. "What part of secret security you don't get Mark? You and frankly with the rest of your team supposed to stay not seen, I see y'all everywhere," Jason said.

"Listen, our job is to protect you and you're paying us very well to do that. You're walking around with a quarter-million casino chips in your hand. I know people who will kill for two-hundred-dollars. So yes, I'm gonna play you close and do my job and so will my team."

"Right, I get it," Jason said knowing he could handle himself. Years of training with Black Ice henchmen he knew he could even take on Mark. *"He just don't know I can probably take half his team out with this bad leg, but it's not civilians I'm concerned about, it's Black Ice. As far as he knows, I died in that compound base with his daughter, so there's no reason for him to think of me or look for me but he's the devil, the last thing I need is to be enjoying myself and he pops up out the shadows ready to put my head in a jar. No thank you, in fact I'm gonna hire even more security. I can never be too safe, but he's not coming to Las Vegas, and I need to push him out my mind before I think him up. Thinking about something or someone too long and they just magically pop up, I don't need that. I'm living my best life. Positive energy and positive thoughts only,"* Jason thought to himself then looked at Mark.

"You know what, you're right and starting tomorrow I want you to increase your team, hire more people and be ready, we're having a party tonight," Jason said as he started walking.

"Daddy wait," Francis said getting up with a cup of coins and running after Jason. The valet handed him the keys and opened the door for him and Francis. They left the casino in his droptop white Ferrari that was waiting for him. Marks team worked fast keeping an eye on him and hopping into black GMC trucks.

Faith sat in the back of a black Mercedes Benz limo with Jainice, Lefty and Cricket. J-Money was in the driver seat. "The information was wrong, it looks like he has a very large security team of twenty three people around the clock," Lefty said while looking at his iPad.

"How is he affording all of this, he's stolen maybe eight-hundred-dollars from my account, looking at his security, cars, and lifestyle he should've burned through that in two or three weeks knowing him," Faith said as they followed the three GMC trucks.

"Well, it looks like he won big at a poker game when he first got here for like thirteen million, and been winning high-stake games and money ever since." Lefty said looking at the articles on the internet.

"So, you getting all that from online, he didn't even bother trying to hide it. He really thought he got away with killing me and his own child, he sold out his own baby for money and the fast life." Faith said out loud.

"Shit people will give their soul and right arm to have a rich lifestyle." Jainice said.

"Yea, he post a lot of pictures on Instagram showing his money and cars." he said. "He got two homes and a penthouse condo." Lefty said.

Faith sat there hurt and mad, *"How could he betray me like that. Why would he want me dead, I loved him? I would've did anything for him."* Faith thought to herself as the car stopped.

"It looks like it's gonna be a party," J-Money said from the front seat.

Faith look out the window. They had stopped at a huge great mansion with a gate in front of it and a security booth. They were checking people i.d's before going in. Cars was lined up down the block, some parking and getting out walking to the to the gates, others driving straight to the gate then driving in.

"This nigga really lost his mind, who the hell he think he is." Lefty said looking at the size of the house and the music's blasting.

"We gonna have to do this another night, when people not around," Jainice said.

"From the information on his social media he has a party every night and let people stay, sleep, fuck, do drugs or whatever based of one of his parties last a week. We could try to get him while going to the casino or leaving but Las Vegas has a lot of police, it's a lot of money out here, so they got to be ready to protect their citizens. Then it was a shooting one year at a hotel, so they been on high alert, but it can be pulled off." Lefty said.

"No!" Faith replied.

"What you mean no, Mistress?" Lefty asked.

"No! We're no gonna wait, we're gonna get him tonight. Call the henchmen get the vans and tractor trailer." Faith replied.

"What? So we gonna take a few people from the party as well? It's a lot of hired people there, we gonna leave them right and take everyone else? That's how Black Ice did it." Lefty said then shut up as he looked in Faith eyes.

"We're taken everyone, now make the call. Get the vans and henchmen here now!" Faith shouted and looked at Lefty as if she would chop his head off.

"Yes." he replied and started making the phone calls.

"We got to get in there before we start the attack but how?" Faith said looking at all the security.

"Girl one thing I know is how to do is crash a party," Jainice said and stepped out the limousine.

"Follow my lead." Faith had on an all-black dress, with diamond crystals on, the dress hugged her body, showing off her voluptuous shape, her hair was done in curls and bounced when she walked. Jainice had on a royal blue dress and her hair in a bun, she walked over to group of men walking to the party. "Me and my girlfriend would love to join you," Jainice said.

The tall slim built guy, looked her up and down then looked at Faith and smiled, "Y'all know these parties get kinda freaky, this no normal party right?" the guy said.

Jainice walked up to him and grabbed his hand then placed his finger in her mouth and began to suck it like it was a dick then pulled it out, "We like freaky." Jainice replied.

"Shit!" the guy said and friends look hyped. "Come on, roll with us," two of them said." Faith stood quiet, her mind raced. The more she thought of her baby's father the more she hated him. She felt like she was in a bad dream as they walked to the front gate and security scanned there i.d and used a metal detector to check for any weapons and let them in. Jainice moved next to Faith as they stood in the group of guys they entered with.

"Listen, I never seen you fucking like this, you're always hard and strong, snap out of

27

whatever going through your mind Boss Lady, you gonna make that nigga pay, but if we fuck up and blow this, he's in the wind and we may never find him again. Put your game face on and be who you are," Jainice said. Faith looked at her and kissed her on the forehead.

"Without you and Lefty I would've lost it already. My father's words just keep playing in my head, telling me not to trust him. That I have to be colder be more like him and he was right. I hate the fact he was right. I was in my own little world, a world that wasn't real. It's the second time I allow that shit to happen to me, but it won't happen again, I swear!" Faith said.

As they entered the house. Music was blasting, it was people walking around handing out drinks and cocaine on a tray like it was normal. The first room was bright, as you walked deeper into the mansion. The other areas had the lights off, and red and blue party lights flashing. People was popping pills and dancing. Faith walked pass some woman sniffing cocaine off a man chest as he lay on the floor. The group of men they entered with walked to the backyard to the pool area where women were jumping up and down. Then Faith looked closely, people was fucking in front of each other.

A guy had his face squeezed between a brown-skin woman ass cheeks eating her pussy and ass from the back. "He turned his house into the sex room," Faith said to Jainice.

"That's definitely what he did." Jainice replied.

"There's got to be over a hundred people in here and more coming, it's look like he added more security," Jainice said as she counted the security guards in suits. Some posted up, others walking around.

"That's not gonna stop shit," Faith said walking off.

"Where you're going?" Jainice asked.

"To find my baby daddy and kill him."

"Fuck!" Jainice said knowing the henchmen wasn't ready yet. She followed Faith into the kitchen, there was people going in and out and one security guard standing by the pantry. Faith seen what she was looking for and grabbed a big knife out the stand.

"Miss! You're not allowed touch the knives," the security guard said.

"Oh, I'm sorry," Faith said and walked toward him and got close to him and stabbed him in the stomach four times. The man stumbled backwards, she open the walking in pantry door and push him in, he was dead before he hit the floor. "Let's go," Faith said shutting the pantry door.

Jainice raised her left eyebrow. "Well, she's back to her damn self at least." Jainice mumbled to herself. As they walked up to the second floor, they walk passed a few rooms with the doors open and people having sex in groups.

Faith watched and waited as one of the guards used a key card to open a thick door. He never noticed Faith storming in the room behind him. Faith sliced his throat, he grabbed his neck, gasping for air and looking at the two guards in the chair watching the tv monitors connected to security cameras all around the property. One of the guards jumped up and stepped around the dead guy and Faith stepped him in the top of his head, the second one she grabbed his face and twisted his neck. She than opened the door for Jainice. "It's time," she said. Faith turned off all security alarms and cameras.

Ten minutes later a knock was at the door, Jainice looked at Faith. "Open it." Jainice opened the door to see Lefty standing there with a duffle bag. "Was there any issues," Faith asked.

"Not really, once you turned off the cameras and alarms, I came in from the backyard. Most of the guards are too busy watching the fucking and I bet the serious ones are guarding Jason so close they can feel him breathe." Lefty replied as he passed Faith the duffle bag.

She opened it, to see her bodysuit and hatchets and dart guns. She held the hatchet in one hand and the dart gun in the next. "Remember what I said, take everyone." Faith said then looked at Jainice after she changed her clothes.

Lefty picked up his phone and said "Begin!" The power on the whole block went out, henchmen jumped out of vans and shot the guards at the front gate, soon as their bodies hit the ground another set of henchmen dragged them to a van. Then twenty henchmen entered the mansion dressed in all black, gave them the cover of night, before anyone could realize what was going on half the security guards and most of the people was shot with darts and knocked out cold because of it.

"Awwww!" a lady screamed as she saw a henchmen running toward her, before she let out another scream a dart hit her in the skull, she lost consciousness right away. A henchmen bust into the bathroom to see a woman on the sink another woman eating her pussy, the two women stopped what they was doing and turned around to see the man dress in all black with a black mask on. "Is this part of role play, if so, we're down, you want us to be the helpless victims and do whatever you say?" The woman that was on her knees said.

Henchmen looked at her confused,

"Both of you get on your knees and crawl to me!" He order.

"Yes daddy! Don't hurt us," the second one said seductively as she pulled down her skirt and got on the floor with her friend and both giggled, looking at each other then slowly and sexually crawled toward him. When they reached him they started to kiss each other, their tongue danced in each other's mouth. They stopped kissing and looked at the henchmen. "What do you want us to do next?" one asked.

The henchmen looked then and pointed the dart gun. "Sleep!" he said.

"Sleep?" one of the women said. "That don't sound very freaky," the other said.

"It wasn't meant to be," the henchmen said squeezing the trigger shooting one in the chest and the other in the face, both women hit the floor face first and losing consciousness.

"Faster!" Lefty ordered as they dragged passed out bodies and placed them into the vans, the vans drove four blocks out the neighborhood, to a waiting eighteen wheeler truck, and threw the bodies in the back of the trailer. People that was partying by the pool area, still had some light shining, and music still going. Not letting the blackout stop them, a woman seen some of the henchmen dragging people out the living room than out the front door, "What the fuck going on?" she said and opened the porch door to only have a dart hit her in the forehead, she started to fall in slow motion forward and a henchmen caught her and dragged her inside the house and out the front door, ten men rushed the backyard. People started to scream but their scream was cut short as darts filled their bodies. Then henchmen grabbed them up as fast as they hit the ground.

Jason laid back while getting head by Francis and watching the five other people in his room fuck, two guys was tagged teaming a woman. She had her mouth full of dick as one hit it from the back. And two women lay on the floor, fucking each other with dildos. Mark stood at the double door and Franky sat in a chair next to him. "Team how long until the power back on? Switch to the emergency generator," Mark said into his headset, but got no answer. "I think my mic dead how about yours?" Mark asked Frank.

Franky shrugged his shoulder. "Team B anyone can hear me?" Franky said and got no answer. "My shit dead too but it could have something to do with the power outage." Franky replied and went back to watching the women having sex on the floor in the master bedroom they was in.

Jason stomach began to bubble, "Get off me!" he shouted pushing Francis off him. He grabbed a sheet then a Glock off the nightstand and got out the bed and walked over to Franky and Mark. "Why is the power still off, we have a generator, if it stay off too long," Jason said.

"I don't know, last I heard the whole block lost power, not just our house so don't worry, you're being paranoid now but in the casino wasn't. We got this," Mark said.

"Yea, but the generator still would've kicked on. Call your team and have them check on it," Jason said then walked to the other side of the large room and looked out the window, and couldn't see nothing but darkness. His hand began to tremble. "He's here! He's here!" Jason said in a panicked voice and ran back over to Mark. "I'm in danger he's here," Jason said grabbing Mark by the collar.

"Relax and who here?" Mark said removing Jason hand. "It's just a black out, it happens all the time you know that," Frank said.

"The devil! The fucking devil here, he knows I killed his daughter and he's coming for me, he's gonna take my fucking head!" Jason shouted and started to cry.

"The devil not real man, just fucking relax, your scaring yourself," Mark said.

"The devil not real, look at my foot," Jason said showing them his left foot that was made of wood, "He took that from me without thinking twice about it, he's gonna put my head in a jar because I betrayed his daughter." Jason said sat in the floor and started rocking back and forth.

", he's tripping talking about the devil and shit." Franky said probably some mushrooms he took.

"You remember last time, he kept seeing the devil," Mark said.

"This isn't like last time, he's coming for me." Jason said.

"Here baby you're probably dehydrated, just need some water in your system," Francis said as he walked across the room with a bottle of water and bent down and tried to hand it to him.

Jason smacked the bottle out of Francis hand. "You're not fucking listening, the devil is here, right now! He's gonna put my head in a jar. I seen the jars with body parts, there's no stopping him. We need to run and find a way out of here," Jason said while crying and could see Black Ice face and his evil eyes and smile in his head.

"Listen you have like a hundred people in this party and I over thirty guards. No one will touch you, if a killer was here, he couldn't get passed all that to get up here without no one calling the police." Mark said.

"Hahahah!" Jason started laughing as if he'd lost his mind. "I was once part of his organization, an organization no one lives to tell about, they move fast and quiet, leaving no witnesses or trace. Rumor was said that the highest governors and government officials along with celebrity benefits from this organization; they help fund the shit for all I know but I wasn't that high up in rank to know that, but when they strike they take everyone. There are cellphone jammers, you can't record, take pictures, or make phone calls. Pull out your phone and try to use it," Jason said.

"Baby your bugging," Francis said and grabbed his phone off the nightstand, and tried to go online and got nothing, he tried to resend a fast video and the phone kept glitching.

Franky pulled out his phone and tried to call someone and nothing happened and the screen turned black. Franky looked at Mark, with a look that said 'oh shit.'

"See he's here. He's the devil, and his organization kidnaps people, sells them, and murder people without a trace, if he kill you they never find your body, you end up in jars or his pets eat you, even your bones. I had his daughter killed and she was just as evil and mean as him. They was devils, the shit they do to people wasn't fucking normal but they'll do it without blinking a fucking eye." Jason said.

"This can't be real, it's a fucking horror story or some shit," Mark said.

"It's a hundred people at this party right?" Jason asked.

"Yea," Mark said as everyone in the room stopped what they was doing and looked at him on the floor and started to get scared.

"So why is it so fucking quiet, our parties don't stop until the next day even with a black out and we pay the neighbors not to call the cops because of the noise," Jason said and started crying again.

Mark eyes opened up wide and his heart started to race, pounding in his chest. "These are just stories that all. I'm gonna check on my team. I can't reach them on the radio," Mark said knowing some of what Jason was saying was true. The whole house was quiet he couldn't even hear people splashing in the pool, nor any moans of pleasure. People would be having sex and taking drugs all through the night but not now. "I'm not gonna let you scare me, I'm gonna do my job and go check on my team," Mark said as he pulled out his long .50 caliber hand gun.

"Your security team is dead or taken there's no one left in this house but us." Jason replied sounding depressed.

"No fucking way anyone can clear out my whole team and everyone in this house without making a sound," Mark said.

"Hahah!" Jason looked at him laughing.

"His daughter once kidnapped four people without making a sound; trust me the shit can be done." Jason said.

"You're using too much drugs," Mark said not wanting to believe him, "You stay here Franky; guard him I'm gonna check on my team, I'm tired of hearing this nonsense," Mark said as he opened the double door and left the door cracked as he let his gun lead the way. He walked down the hallway, he could barely see. He looked into the rooms as he passed them and could see they was completely empty, nothing was there just beds, no clothes or anything. "What the fuck is going on here?" he said as he walked down another flight of stairs.

Franky stood up and pulled out his Glock .45 and gripped it tight. "Was all the stories you just said true? There's really a guy that chops people heads off and put them in jars? Franky asked. He was a big Italian man with black hair and weighed close to three hundred pounds, he had a dark blue suit on and a white button shirt underneath.

The other five people in the room started to get dressed. "I think we should leave," one of the women said.

"Yes everything true, you're about to find out and I wouldn't leave if I was you," Jason said.

"I'm out of here," a Spanish woman with blonde hair said that had her body done. She put on her dress and ran out the room. "Ahhhh! Ahh! Ahhh!" five second later, her screams mix with Marks screams through the quiet house.

"I told you he's here." Jason said and got up from the floor and ran toward the bathroom door. He stood there with his gun aimed at the master bedroom double door. "Shut the door Jason said when the screams stopped.

"That was Mark, why was he screaming? Mark is one of the toughest men I know, he don't even cry, shit he was in the army and now a veteran. He wouldn't just scream like that," Franky said now even more scared.

"I said shut the fucking door!" Jason screamed while crying.

Franky moved to push to door close then stopped when something hit the floor hard, sounding like a rock and rolled into the room, then it happened a second tone. Franky use the flashlight on his gun and shined it down at the first object. It looked like a big ball with long hair on it. Franky bent down and moved the hair around to see it was the young woman who had just ran out the room, her eyes was open and so was her mouth.

"Ahhh!" the other four people in the room screamed when they seen it. Franky backed up scared, then looked at the next ball that rolled in the room to see it was Mark's head.

"Ahhhh! Ahhh!! Jason screamed looking at the heads, He's here!!!!" The room door bust open and Jason ran into the bathroom with Francis behind him, shutting the door.

Franky aimed and squeezed the trigger five times, as someone entered the room, he was sure he hit the person but someone grabbed his arm and he screamed as it was chop off, then he felt a sharp pain in his neck as someone kept swinging, cutting through the fat of his neck until it came completely detached and rolled off his body. The four people in the room scream as men ran toward them swinging with blood and body parts went flying everywhere. One of the women hid up under the bed as a guy she was fucking was sitting on the floor begging for his lift. "No please! Please don't kill me," the man begged.

The woman heard a voice say. "I thought you was gonna take them all," then a woman replied "Not them." Then the head split open into two, he fell sideways and his brain fell out his skull. His eyes seemed as if he was still alive as he looked at the woman up under the bed. Another woman ran toward the bedroom door, a hatchet flew in the air and hit her in the back, her legs got weak and dropped straight to the floor. "I can't move! Why I can't move?" the woman cried out as she kept telling her body "Get up! Get up!" the woman said out loud as her mind kept telling her body to get up and run, but her body wouldn't listen. She could hear footsteps behind her, "Ahhh!" she screamed as the hatchet was pulled out her back, and a newfound pain traveled through her body, she tried to scream but couldn't as her head was detached and rolled away, she was still alive and look at her own body with her head no longer on it before her brain died.

The woman under the bed tried to fight back her tears, she covered her mouth with her hands to keep from screaming. She could still hear footsteps walking around the bed. "Go away! Go away just go away!" the woman said in her head and started praying. Then felt a hand on her ankle. "Ahhhh!" She screamed as she was pulled up from under the bed and the hatchet started to chop chunks off the back of her neck, before she could scream again her head was chopped off.

"Collect all the heads," a voice said.

Jason looked around panicking thinking what to do, he could hear footsteps coming toward the bathroom door. He aimed and squeezed the trigger. Francis screamed with each shot as the bullets went through the bathroom door, Jason continued to squeeze the trigger of the gun until he heard a clicking sound.

"Did you get that daddy? Did you get them?" Francis asked.

"There's no stopping the devil, only slowing him down," Jason said as he opened the bathroom windows and looked down at the pool, he was three stories up. "Fuck, climb out or die, climb," he said to himself as he started to climb out the window.

"Wait, don't leave me baby," Francis said as he peeped his head out the window to see Jason shimmy down to the second floor, grabbing whatever he could, to get down, window ledges, bricks, or whatever. Francis started to climb out and felt someone grab both his legs. "Daddy help! Help!" he screamed looking out the window and holding on to the window ledge for dear life.

Jason looked up just as Francis was snatched back inside the bathroom. He let out around girly piercing scream. Then it was nothing, just silence. "Shit!" Jason said knowing he didn't have much time. He climbed down to the first floor and jumped, he looked inside the house and could see henchmen inside just standing there watching him with their black mask on. He ran around the pool and jump over the fence and could see more henchmen standing down the street but none of them attacked him or moved an inch. They just looked at him as he ran down the block.

"What the fuck is going on, why they didn't touch me?" Jason thought and turned around to look only to see something flying toward him but it was too late for him to duck as something hit him in the head, it felt hard as a rock. He fell face

first onto the street. He fought to keep his eyes open, as the object that hit him in the head rolled next to his face. "Ahhh!" he screamed as he looked at Francis head. His eyes were closed but his mouth was wide open as if he was still trying to scream. "Francis baby I'm sorry, Francis," Jason said while crying. He was trying to get up then felt the sting of two darts hit his back making him lose consciousness instantly.

The sound of crying made Jason open his eyes, his head was throbbing like someone hit him with a rock, then he remembered he got hit with Francis skull. "Francis," he said crying out loud as he rubbed the back of his head. He slowly sat up and looked at his feet to see they was chained, then realized he was moving. He looked around and knew exactly where he was at, people from his party was knocked out on the floor. Some was waking up crying and pulling on the chains. *Shit I'm in the trailer,* Jason thought to himself as the trailer stopped and the back opened up, two henchmen dressed in all black with black mask on climbed in.

"Help! Help us!" one woman screamed while another one shouted, "Let me free please, let the fuck go." The henchmen raise their dart guns and started shooting everyone in the trailer knocking them back out. A young white guy screamed. "Please don't, I have money I'll pay you, I'm rich.

Don't do this!" but before he could scream anything else a dart hit him in the chest and he passed out on top of another person.

Jason raise his hands up as a henchmen stood in front of him. "Wait, I'm one you guys, they're been a misunderstanding. I'm loyal to Black Ice," Jason said. The henchmen kicked him in the face.

"We know who you are traitor, I lost friends because of you, but you'll get yours." The henchmen said raising his dart gun.

"No! There's some misunderstanding. I'm loyal to Black Ice," Jason said as a dart hit him in the center of his forehead and he lost consciousness. The smell of urine made his nose itch, "Ugh, what the fuck?" Jason moaned. "Fuck those darts are worse than drinking dark liquor all night. "Why my head feel like this?" Jason said and tried to touch his head but couldn't. "What the fuck going on?" he said out loud and forced opened his eyes. He looked around and could see he was in a dark room with one light on and further looking down to see that he was in a steel chain that had been drilled to the floor and his legs were strapped to the legs of the chair and his arms were strapped down on the arm rest.

Jason tried to wiggle free but couldn't. The sound of a chain rattling behind him made him jump, "Who there?" Jason asked, but got no answer. But the sound of something walking toward him but it made a clicking sound with each step. "Fuck I'm gonna get feed to hyenas," Jason cried but sounded more like whining. *At least it will be fast, I lived the life I wanted. Finally got to see what it's like to be rich.*" Jason thought to himself as the door bust open but he couldn't see who was coming in the room because it was too dark. "Whatever anyone say it's a lie, I'm loyal Black Ice," Jason screamed.

"You're not loyal to no one but yourself." Jason heard a voice say and his heart sunk to his stomach, and his stomach started bubbling up with fear then he passed gas, letting lose stinky ass farts as Faith stepped into the light holding a jar. She put the jar on the floor in front of him. Jason looked down, "Francis" he cried out and Faith punched him in the face.

"You cry over that man you just met but not me or you child," Faith said and punched him again in the eye then the nose. "You was gay the whole fucking time? My father tried to warn me about you so did the others, I trusted you," Faith said punching him in the mouth. "I loved you, I gave myself to your light-skin ass. I told you about my past, the pain, the betrayal, and you turn around and do the same fucking thing? Fuck, even worse! Antonio sent his sons to rape me, you told people where we was so they can kill me while I was carrying your child!" Faith screamed and punching him repeatedly in the jaw then nose, his nose broke and blood gushed out. Faith then punched him in the neck. "I don't know what hurt more, catching you getting fucked by another man, seeing you suck dick like I use to suck yours, or the fact this all was a big ass game to you," Faith said punching him the neck again.

"Baby wait, stop I'm sorry. I have demons, I can't help it, I like men and gambling. It's my demons inside me, I love you!" Jason said.

"Don't you fucking baby me. You got demons? Bitch you have no idea what real demons are. I thought with you, the baby and Ella-Ana I had everything I wanted. The urge to kill would stop and it did a little, I thought I wouldn't have to be like my father. I had more than enough money a family, friends and you and that bitch fucked it up. You want to see what a demon inside you looks like?" Faith said, then opened the jar with Francis head in it and grabbed it by the hair. She held on tight to it like a purse then started swinging it. "You fucking asshole, if you was gay you could've said so!" she screamed.

With each swing, the head connected with Jason's face and it felt like he was getting beaten with a brick. "Ahhh! Ahh stop! I'm sorry, Ahhhh!

Stop please, stop!" Jason cried as his cheekbone broke.

"Did you know? Did you know?" Faith shouted between hitting him with the skull.

"Did I know what?" Jason cried out.

Faith stopped for a second to breathe. She looked at Jason in the chair butt naked. His face badly beaten and blood gushing out of it.

"Did you know that bitch was gonna take our baby?" Faith ask while trying not to cry.

"What, no I didn't know. She just said if I tell her husband where the base was I wouldn't have to worry about you no more." Jason replied.

"In other words kill me and you child!" Faith shouted and hit him with the head twice. "Ahhhugg, please stop. I can't take any more." Jason begged.

"Why did you do it? I need answers I need closure, why pretend like you love me for almost a year, get me pregnant to rob me and have someone kill me and your child?" Faith said staring at him not understanding.

Jason spit out blood on the floor, blood dripped out his nose, making it hard for him to breathe.

"I'll tell you everything if you promise not to beat me no more and just kill m , get it over with," Jason said.

Faith looked at him and put the head back in the jar with water. "Speak," she said. Looking at him deeply a part of her still loved him, flashbacks of him holding her at night, Kissing her forehead in the morning played in her mind. How he use to rub her stomach when the baby was kicking, how he made love to her. Tears slowly came out the corner of her eyes. She sat down on the floor in front of him Indian style. "I'm waiting," Faith said.

"I can't breathe, give me a second please. Jason said in pain as he sucked the blood in his nostrils up then spit it out on the floor. He exhale and inhale deeply. His jaw felt as it was broken. He was sure both his cheekbones was, but knew if he didn't talk Faith would beat him to death and the process was going to be slow and painful, feeling every blow.

"I've always been gay but a street nigga, so I couldn't come out like that, but when you bought men to the sex room that you kidnapped shit, 20% of the henchmen that work for Black Ice came out and I just happen to be one of them. It was like, fuck it." Jason said then looked at her as if she was going to jump up and hit him. "You gonna kill me anyway, so I'm gonna speak freely. Your father chopped off my fucking left foot!" Jason shouted weekly.

"I know and I saved your life after and had you work for me when he wanted you dead cause you was scared to fight." Faith said still not understanding.

"You don't get it, your father chopped off my left foot and put it in a jar. I was helpless. I can't beat Black Ice, shit who can? Shit, you're the only one I seen hit him and got away with it. I heard stories of his sons that came close to killing him but that was before my time. Yes, you saved my life but you really think I could let go of someone making me handicap for the rest of my life? I had to learn to re-walk, sit up, I would never run again or play baseball, so yes I was bitter and petty. When I seen that you liked me, the best revenge I could ask for was to fuck the daughter of the man I despised. Hell yea, I jumped to the opportunity and fuck the shit out of you with hate not love, every time I was inside you I thought of your father and how much I hated him. Then you started to trust me, showing me your overseas bank accounts, I couldn't believe you had all of them. But I remembered you telling me, you was stuck in a room most of your life because people or women don't do that shit, no matter if they are dating they keep some shit secret but you was like an open book. Deep down I wanted to kill you but knew I

50

couldn't get away with it, you just ended up pregnant. When you locked me in the cell after you caught me cheating, and Ella-Ana set me free and gave me your laptop all for me to give her husband the location I felt like I hit the lottery, and I did. I gambled your money, turned it into millions of dollars and lived my best life in three months, partying, drinking, fucking, being the man, had luxury cars and homes, it was all worth it Faith. I didn't think you'd live to be honest. I thought your father was coming for me. That somehow he found out I survive the massacre on the compound because I was living too loud, to be real, I'll do it all again." Jason said.

Faith cried silently for a second then wiped her tears and stood up. "I see and understand, my father said a hard head would make a soft ass, that I liked to learn the hard way. It's so fucking hard when your dad right about a man or anything when you want him to be wrong," Faith said and started to laugh. Jason stared her in the eyes.

"Get on with it. Finish me off," Jason said. Faith smirked her devilish smile and all Jason could see was her father and a chill went up his spine, and his heart raced. Faith walked behind him, he tried to turn around too but couldn't. He heard what sounded like a cage opening, then footsteps that clicked on the floor. The lights in the room turned on, making the room bright like a hospital. He could see the floor was all porcelain and white. He looked at Francis head in the jar and wanted to cry all over again, but heard Faith walking around him. She now stood in front of him holding a leash. Jason's eyes followed down on the leash to see Regina, Faith's mother with a gag ball in her mouth, her limps had been chopped off, she had some kind of hard plastic on them, to help her keep pressure on what was left of her legs and arms. She moved around on all four limps like a short bull dog.

Faith held the leash and pulled her mother walking her around Jason in a circle, she's like my own personal dog but even better, "I bust one of her ear drums, now she makes even funnier sounds when she tries to talk with no tongue, watch," Faith said then unstrapped the gag ball.

Regina moved around her mouth then opened to speak. "Ugh ahhhh! Ahhh!" she made a weird sound, kinda like a mute person when they try to speak. They can't hear the tone of their voice but with no tongue. Jason looked at Regina and could see the pain in her eyes. Hell Faith had shaved all her hair off, and she was still overweight and looked like a trap sea lion on a leash.

Faith stuffed the gag ball back in her mouth and the room door opened. J-Money stepped in with Lefty and a nurse in a green uniform and equipment in her hand. Faith passed the leash to Lefty, who took Regina back to the cage. "You remember what I did to my mother? You was there and looked like you was gonna vomit, well that's what I'm gonna do with you," Faith said with an evil smile on her face that Jason had never seen before and her eyes scared the hell out of him that he lost control of his bowels and shitted on himself.

"Wait no! You promised you'd kill me! Just kill me, chop me up and put me jars! Don't you dare break your promise!" Jason shouted in fear. Faith grabbed a long chrome needle off the tray the nurse was holding and sat down on Jason's lap. "You said you was gonna kill me bitch, kill me! I'm happy they took your baby hoe! I never liked your pussy, I can't stand pussy and you made me hate it even more!" Jason shouted hoping to get a reaction out of her, making her mad enough to end his life. But Faith just continue to smile that sick evil grin as Lefty stood behind Jason and grabbed his head so he couldn't move it.

"No, let me gooo. Kill me! Y'all better fucking kill me!" he shouted while trying to move his head from left to right. He hopped around in the chair but didn't go nowhere because of the straps and the fact the chair was bolted to the floor. Faith looked him dead in the eyes as she pushed the needle into his right ear. "Ahh stop! Bitch stop!"

he screamed as she pushed it deeper, she didn't stop until she seen blood. "No!" Jason said but his words sounded funny, he couldn't hear out his right ear no more. It was like a piercing ringing sound in that ear then nothing. "What you do to me?" he said but sounded funny talking. He then spit in Faith's face.

She wiped the spit off her face with two fingers then sucked it. "Read my lips, you really think spit gonna bother me or upset me, you use to cum on my face baby," Faith said still smiling like the cat and swallowed as J-Money walk over and grabbed Jason's cheeks and squeezed his mouth open. Faith pulled out a knife from her holster and dug in his mouth and grabbed his tongue and slowly started to slice at it, as if she was using a saw to cut a tree until she cut it all the way off and threw it in the jar with Francis head.

She got off him and stood up as blood pour out of his mouth. The nurse passed Faith a blue cloth. Faith wipe her hands as the nurse stepped closer and J-Money kept Jason's mouth open. "This gonna hurt," the nurse said as she pulled out a thread and needle and started stitching up his tongue. "This gonna hurt a lot. The boss lady said no pain killers for you until two days, and that's just to keep you alive and heal from all of this but she wants you to feel everything. It's funny because you was there when I did the first one?

Funny how the roles switch." The nurse said as she finished up and stepped back waiting for the next step.

"I would think we're getting better at this. I think after one more time we'll have this mastered. I'm actually timing this, want to see how fast we can complete this," Faith said looking at Jason crying with his face all beat up, blood dripping out his mouth mixed with drool and blood dripping out his ear.

"Kill me!" Jason tried to say but it didn't sound nothing like that.

"I know what you're trying to say, but it will never happen, you tried to kill me and our child. That's the lowest shit a man can do but since I love you, you'll be my pet, I'll keep you forever. You'll never be too far from me; when I get stress I'll be able to sit down and talk to you. It works wonders for me and my mother, she can never scream, "I should've flushed you down the toilet" no more. She just lays there like a dog by my feet crying while I tell her how my day was. This the closest we've ever been and I love it. I can't wait for us to be that close," Faith said as Jainice entered the room holding Faith's chrome double blade axe and walked over and passed it to her.

"Nooo! Nooo!" Jason cried uncontrollably.

"Don't cry baby, this can't hurt more than someone cutting your stomach open and ripping your baby out of you or being crushed to death under a fucking building for three weeks. Oh, did I mention the flesh eating roaches? Yea, they had flesh eating roaches, they must've really hated my ass, but you don't have to go through none of that baby cause I love you!" Faith said and swung the axe chopping off his right leg just above the knee cap. Jainice turned on the blow torch and heated up the axe in Faith's hand. Faith then pressed it against the now open wound.

"Ahhh! Ughh!" Jason screamed as the hot metal burned his flesh. He couldn't take it no more and passed out losing consciousness. The nurse pulled out a syringe with a long needle and walked over to Jason and jammed the needle into his chest and pushed the liquid inside him. "Ugh!" Jason gasped for air and woke up and prayed it was all a dream, but it wasn't, he could feel the pain all over his body again but now he felt as if he snorted ten grams of cocaine at once. He was as hyper as a crackhead or a five-year-old eating too much chocolate.

"You really are a bitch, my dad said don't trust no light-skin man, y'all soft as hell but I refused to believe him. Like look daddy, he got tattoos on his face, he's a thug. Turned out to be a cry baby, bottom feeder, dick sucker, using my tricks on the next man. You know I chopped off three of my mother's limbs before she passed out, or was it two? I can't recall but I know her old crackhead ass didn't pass out from me chopping one limb, like damn you had your foot cut off, you should be use to this. You should be a man with pride and stop all the screaming and crying for God sake's. I'm really looking down at you, you changed my whole perspective of you, shit even when I hated you, you still was a man in my eyes not a punk. This whole time you been crying, screaming, shitting on yourself, yes I know you shitted on yourself. We all know and can smell it, and the green shit dripping off the side of the chair. What the fuck wrong with you, take this shit like a man and to think I got to call you my baby father," Faith said and swung again this time chopping off his left leg above the knee.

Jason screamed "Uughahhhh!" Faith rolled her eyes as Jainice heated up the axe. She started pressing it against his leg. "Stop! Stop no more! No more, I can't take no more." Jason tried to scream but it didn't sound nothing like that as Faith pulled the axe away from his burning flesh. I think you're starting to feel the pain I went through baby and that's a good thing. We'll be able to look back at this one day and really understand how we hurt each other, who knows maybe even forgive," Faith said. "Naw, I'll never forgive you," Faith said as her eyes opened up wide and she swung down chopping off his right arm just under the elbow.

"You know I have to get it just right, if I cut off too much or leave too much when you walk on all fours you'll be off balance, it's really a skill. You got to eye the cut, I can always use a marker, but fuck that, I really think I'm getting better at this." Faith said as she placed the hot axe to his arm.

All Jason could do was cry. *"Why won't she kill me? just kill me please. I want to die."* Jason thought to himself as he cried out in excruciating pain. He had snot mix with blood dripping out his nose and drool coming out his mouth onto his chest, his body was shaking from the pain he was in.

"Can he die?" Faith asked the nurse.

She ran over to his left arm and took his blood pressure and looked back at Faith. "Yes, he can't handle the pain unlike your mother, he can go into shock and die. You're not gonna be able to go days without pain medication with him. Shit, I'm not sure if you take his next arm he may not make it, he might just die. His heart all over the place and blood pressure too high." the nurse replied.

"What if he was unconscious, could I finish then and you give him pain medicine to the pussy and antibiotics would he be okay then? Faith asked.

"Yes, but he would need maybe three weeks to a month until you wake him up. He would need to sleep while his body heals, I think it was different for your mother's case. If you don't mind, may I speak freely Mistress?" the nurse asked.

"Go head," Faith said holding the axe tight wandering if she would have to take the nurse head off if she said something she didn't like.

"Your mother was able to handle the pain better because she was on drugs and she'd been tortured before by your father, a normal person can't handle the pain, their body will shut down, killing them, thinking it's actually saving them." the nurse stated.

"Okay, that's not an issue we can work around that." Faith said then leaned in to Jason and kiss him on the forehead. "I think I needed you to cross me, to wake me up from the dream I was living in, the pain hurted more than I could bare, pretty much how you feeling. The only thing is your pain will stop one day, mine will always be in my heart, there to remind me. But I no longer seek love or the validation of others, it has helped me embrace the evil in me the serial killer in me, the devil in me and truly love it. You destroyed my heart and any weakness in me. I love it, I feel stronger, yes at moments I feel sad and get down but it goes away. I think because I wasn't really trying to stand on my own. I needed others to hold me up. I don't feel like that no more. You probably won't understand what I'm talking about. I just wanted to think before you take your nap baby." Faith said not sure if it got through to Jason.

He was squirming in the chair. Shaking and crying hysterically. Faith pulled out a dart gun and shot him in the chest and he instantly stop moving and lost consciousness. Then she swung the axe chopping off his left arm just under his elbow. Jainice heated the axe and Faith press it against his flesh, stopping the bleeding.

The nurse quickly rushed over and stuck an i.v in his left arm that push fluids and antibiotics into his system. Then an i.v in his right arm, pumping fresh blood into his body. "Get more people in this. Bring whoever you need from the medical team. Keep him alive, if he die, you'll take his place. J-Money grab Francis," Faith ordered as she looked at Jason slumped in the chair, knocked out with no legs and no arms. She smiled, it reminded her of her childhood when she would catch spiders and pull off their legs and they would still be alive or she'll catch a fly and pull off its wings. And her favorite was catching the roaches when she was bored and pulled their legs off one by one and kept them in jails for months and they was still alive, now she can pull limbs off, something bigger and keep them alive. Faith smiled and walked away.

Jason was at the poker table, and looked at his hand, and he was going to win, he looked at every one at the table and behind him he could see Francis on the slot machines. "Why does this feel like déjà vu, like I did this all before, it's so weird?" Jason thought to himself as he threw down the cards and said "Full house." and won. The dealers pushed more than $500,000 in casinos chips toward him. He grabbed them and could see Mark his security guard following close behind him, as he walked outside and Francis was by his side. Jason seen a woman standing across the street, something about her caught his attention. She was just standing there looking straight at him, no movement. He squinted his eyes to get a better look and seen Faith's face.

"Oh God, she's here. The devil's daughter is here she's here. Mark get the team," Jason said while crying, he turned around to look at Mark. Mark smiled at him then his head slid off his body and rolled to the floor and blood gushed out his neck like a fire hydrant. "Oh God!" Jason screamed then turned to Francis "Baby, we got to run!" Jason screamed then Francis head slid off his body as well. "Noooo!" Jason hollered then

opened his eyes to see Francis lying next to him.
"Shit it was all a dream," Jason said closing back
his eyes. "Francis baby, I had the worse dream
ever, that my crazy baby mother came back alive
and was waiting for us at the casino." Jason said
then heard the words that came out his mouth, and
it sounded nothing like it did in his head.

"What the fuck!" he thought to himself as he
opened his eyes fully and could see Francis lying
next to him, but then realized Francis was in a jail.
"Ahh!" Jason tried to scream and sit up but kept
falling down, "Calm down! Calm down, this is just
another dream," Jason said laying on his back with
his eyes closed. *"Take deep breaths and open your*
eyes and you'll be back in your mansion, with your
nice cars. I must've ate too many mushrooms last
night that's why I'm tripping and got lock jaw,
that's all." Jason thought to himself as he tried to
open his mouth to speak but couldn't.

He opened his eyes once more and his heart
started to race, he could see Francis head clear as
day in a glass jar with water in it floating, looking
right at him. Jason tried to sit up but couldn't,
trying to use his arms but that didn't work. He
looked down at his arms to see they had been
chopped off and now had a hard plastic over it,
covering it. *"Fuck going on here?"* Jason thought
to himself why rolling off his back and tryna stand
up with no hands, but fell to his face. He looked

down and his legs was gonna, and the same plastic cover that was on his arm.

He looked around his environment, he was in a tall cage, in a room, there was a cage next to his and someone was moving around. "What is that? What going on?" Jason thought to himself and used his back and he scooped inch by inch using his back and ass muscle to get close to the cage. He exhale when he reached it and looked inside. He could see Regina on all fours. Using the plastic cups that covered her missing limbs to walk around and drinking water out a dog bowl. Regina turned and looked at him, despair and sadness was all in her eyes. She turned away and went back to drinking water out the bowl. Everything started rushing back to Jason. An imagine of Faith chopping off his limbs and cutting out his tongue and making him deaf in one ear. *"It wasn't a dream, It wasn't a dream."* Jason thought to himself as he rolled off his back and stood on all four of his limbs like a dog as the room door opened and Faith walked in with a smile on her face.

"Good you're up, you been sleeping for a month now, I thought I was gonna have to kill the medical staff a few times, you caught a fever a few times, and look you already learned how to stand and walk, it took my mother two months to get it. She kept trying to stand up, now you're a pet now," Faith said as she walked closer to the cage to get a better look at him. "I left your boyfriend head in there, thinking it would give you comfort when you woke up. I hoped it worked," Faith said.

Jason started crying, like he never cried before and opened his mouth to talk but the words didn't come out, just funny animal sounds, like a giraffe calling for help or a crying sheep. "Kill me! Kill me!" Jason tried to say but couldn't get the words out. He then walked to the far end of the cage then ran into the bars of the cage and felt nothing. He ran back to the other end of the cage and tried again.

"Yea, that's not gonna work baby , my mother tried it, the cage is made of plastic, you can't really hurt yourself. I got henchmen watching y'all on camera 24/7 for suicide watch. My mother tried many ways to kill herself, she even tried not to eat. I'm dying for you to try that one, but keep trying, the more you try to kill yourself the more I can learn and improve. I heard people that get life in jail try to kill themselves all the time and are never successful. They're forced to do the time no matter what. I learn so much from reading. I'm gonna enjoy the time we will spend together baby. I actually miss you and I been stressing wondering what that bitch is doing to our child, is she or even still alive? Is she beating she mor he, like a Regina did m? Did they sale he or she? I don't even know if it's a boy or girl. But I promise you baby, they will pay, everyone that hurt me will pay," Faith said while smiling.

"They'll regret betraying me," Faith said while she touched her stomach and looked down at it, then back up at Jason. "Sometime I can still feel the baby kicking, I read somewhere when you lose a major part of you, you still feel it there, like your arms and legs, I bet you felt like they was still there. It's was nice talking to you but I have work to do baby daddy and welcome to the zoo!" Faith said as she turned around and walked away leaving Jason screaming and crying, making a weird sound.

"Ughhrrrr! Ugrrrrr!" Jason scream with no tongue looking at Faith's back.

Chapter 4

Meashell sat at the dinner table with her half-bother, "Stop looking like that I told you already you're safe here little Sis, no one will ever find you here. Molokai is an island most people from the states never visit. They don't think of the other islands of Hawaii." Akoni said. He was dark brown-skin complexion and over three hundred pounds. He look like he could be related to The Rock but most Hawaiians are massive men and Akoni fits that description. "Everyone in this village is your family somehow in some way. You're safe here, my bothers Haku and Kahle are ruthless and great with any weapon. No one will ever kidnap you again," Akoni said.

"You don't understand brother, these people are trained. They train every day like there in the Army and their leader is like a demon. The things he does isn't normal." Meashell replied.

"Here drink this," Laka, Akoni's wife said giving Meashell a cup of tea.

"I get you been through the worst but it's over baby sister, you escaped and you said that you watched the woman that kidnapped you die." Akoni replied.

Meashell took the cup of the tea, Leka's tea always relaxed her and got her high at the same time. Flashbacks of her and Minglee running from the compound as it was attacked and falling apart. Then an image of her kicking Faith in the face then the ribs as she bled to death and Jainice trying to protect her as the building came down on them. Meashell snapped back to reality. "Yes, she's dead but her father is out there. I don't think he ever paid any real attention to me but it scares me, like P.T.S.D. I'm traumatized because of that shit, a part of me thinks I should've left with Minglee, like I'm putting y'all in danger," Meashell said.

"Nonsense, your half African and Hawaiian but our father raised you. We're your family and got your back, you're safe here and can start over. The mainland and states aren't for us," Akoni said and was interrupted.

"Auntie! Auntie!" two girls came running up to Meashell and hugged her, then a third one came up to hug her. Meashell smiled looking at her three nieces. Kamea was twelve and the oldest, always kept her hair in a ponytail, and look like her father. Lani was the six-years-old and the youngest and the one that hugged her leg. Kaia was the loudest always and nine-years-old.

"Can we go fishing tomorrow?" Kaia asked.

"Yes auntie! Can we?" Lani asked.

"Yes babies, we can go," Meashell said smiling. *"Damn where would I be without these girls, I swear they make everything better. I thank you God for them and my family,"* Meashell thought to herself.

Meashell looked at the long table full of food, the night sky was beautiful, you could see the stars. Eating outside was normal to her family, the village they lived in was small, no more than sixty homes with families, but everyone ate together, at long tables next to the beaches. Torches lit up the night and fire pits with two wild pigs being roasted, and most of the older women in the village were cooking in the kitchen. The women would bring the food to the table while the men all sat around the fire laughing and talking. "To think, I left this to go to New York thinking this was better. How stupid and foolish I was, I know better now. Family is everything," Meashell said as more people started to sit at the table.

Meashell niece sat next to her and smiled at her. "Why y'all keep looking at me like that?" Meashell asked.

The girls giggled then Kaia said the loudest, "Because you're so pretty, we like your skin, it's like chocolate and the way you smell auntie. We hope to grow up as pretty as you are auntie," Kaia said.

"And strong, don't forget strong," Kamea the oldest said.

"Yea auntie, you should take us hunting with you one day this week," Lani said.

"Girl you just a baby, you're not ready for all that, just continue going to the store for what you need, one day we'll go hunting," Meashell said as her brother Akoni sat down next to his wife.

The table started to fill up with all the families as the women brought more food to the table to eat. Meashell couldn't help but to feel at peace, for once her mind wasn't all over the place. It was eight tables outside and everyone was eating and laughing. The high school girls and boys came and put on a show dancing by the fire as music blasted. When they finally stopped dancing, Meashell stood up with a cup full of Hawaiian rum, "Excuse me," she said and everyone stopped and looked in her direction. Meashell looked at all the tables and began to speak, "It's been years since I been home, I thought by being in the big city I found something better, lived the fast life, more like the luxury life they posted on the internet, I learn the hard way that's not the life for me. I've been home four months now and never been so happy. I'm thankful to be back in my village and thankful for the love y'all have shown and gave me, makes me realize family is everything," Meashell said then heard clapping behind her and a voice that sent chills down her spine. Her legs started trembling and she feared turning around.

"I couldn't say it better, family is everything," Faith said then tossed something hard on the table. It rolled for a second then stop in front of Akoni, Meashell's brother.

Akoni looked at what the woman threw on the table then screamed "Aahhhhh Haku! Haku!" Akoni scream looking at his brother's decapitated head looking at him. Meashell slowly turned around to see Faith standing there with a bloody hatchet in her hand, with Jainice standing next to her and henchmen dressed in all black and black masks. "Run!" Meashell shouted.

"No, we fight!" Akoni screamed as everyone started scrambling from the tables. Akoni ran to a hut and started passing out rifles, guns and bow and arrows to the men then the women. A few of the men from the village aimed their rifles at Faith and her henchmen and sent a hail of bullets toward them, the bullets bounced off the henchmen masks and body.

"That's not gonna work!" Meashell shouted. "You have to shoot them in the eye." Meashell said as a henchmen ran up to her with a dart gun. She grabbed his wrist, twisted it then flipped him to the ground and placed his head between her legs and twisted real fast, snapping his neck.

"Auntie a super hero," Lana said from up under the table with her sisters. Meashell spin kicked another henchmen and grabbed the gun out his holster and lifted up his mask and shot him in the face.

"Looks like someone took their training seriously," Faith said to Jainice.

"Yea, we had to train twice as hard as the men, we was the only female henchmen and you know how guys look at women as if they're weak. You know that you pushed us to the limit, so you can't be too surprised she's gonna beat these guys asses without breaking a sweat. It's gonna take one of us to take her down." Jainice replied.

"I'm not surprised, you know I'm all women power, so it's just fun to watch, but I can't let her kill too many of our people," Faith said as Meashell side stepped as a dart flew at her and she ran up to two henchmen, she front kick one and swept kicked the other knocking him off his feet.

She kicked off their face masks and shot both of them in the face. "She's good," Faith said smiling.

"Shit Minglee even better. Two years of straight combat training made all of us into weapons," Jainice said.

"Not Jason," Faith said and started laughing as more henchmen rushed from behind her and started running down on the beach shooting people with darts, then grabbed their bodies as they hit the sand.

"Stop them from taking our people!" Akoni shouted as he shot two of the henchmen in the chest. They didn't fall down. Then he looked down the beach to see Meashell shooting them in the eyes or lifting there mask up then shooting them in the head. He seen a henchmen dragging a woman across the sand, he ran up to him and punch him in the stomach, knocking all the air out his lungs. The henchmen bent over gasping for air and Akoni snatched his mask off and shot him in the top of the skull.

Akoni turned around to see his bother Kahle fighting off five henchmen at once. His massive size made the henchmen look like little boys as he kicked them up and threw them across the beach.

"J-Money handle him," Faith said looking at Kahle.

J-Money ran up to Kahle and stopped. They studied each other up and down. Kahle looked like a true Hawaiian with his shirt off and body covered in tribal tattoos along with his long curly hair down to his back. He was over three-hundred pounds of muscle, built like a football player. He looked at J-Money who was far from a small man at 6'2 tall and two-hundred-fifty pounds. "So they finally sent a man to fight me, no more of the tiny baby men, huh?" Kahle said and another henchmen ran up on him and Kahle grabbed him and snapped his neck. "The tiny men don't eat enough," Kahle said.

"I agree," J-Money said as he took off his face mask then charged Kahle. Their arms locked, holding each other while trying to pick each other up. Kahle head butted J-Money in the nose then the eye then broke their embrace and twisted his arm and broke it. He then lifted up J-Money and raised him up over his head then slammed him down on his knee with all his might. A cracking sound could be heard as J-Money back broke, Kahle then tossed J-Money to the floor as if he was nothing with his back broken and twisted up. Kahle kicked him in the face. "I guess you not so big after all," Kahle said and turned his back, leaving J-Money on the ground. Kahle grabbed two henchmen by the head and slammed their heads into each other, the blow was so powerful it knocked them out instantly.

Meashell ran over to her brother, "We need to get out of here, we can't win this. They will keep coming, bring more men and eventually overpower us." Meashell said.

"No we don't run , this is our home. We will fight for it like our ancestors did!" Akoni shouted.

"Keep fighting! Keep fighting! You're not getting it. Look," Meashell said pointing to the people that got knocked out by darts, now being dragged away. Meashell counted seven getting taken to the road and being put in vans.

"We will get our people back and call to the other villages to help." Akoni replied.

"There technology is better, all we can do is run, grab your family brother and run, listen to me please," Meashell said then stop talking as something caught her eye and Akoni.

They watched as J-Money twisted around on the sand then lay straight with his hands on his side and got back up. "His back was broken, how did he get up just now?" Akoni asked with a confused look on his face.

"I don't know," Meashell said then looked over at Faith and Jainice. *"The last time she seen Faith, she was cut open and shot, but she was standing over there like nothing happened at all, and I know the building fell on her and Jainice. Me and Minglee stood outside and watched. They supposed to be dead, all three of them,"* Meashell thought to herself.

J-Money walked over to Kahle and tapped him on the shoulder. Kahle turned around and seen J-Money, "But how?" he said as J-Money punch him in the mouth, then the eye. He then grabbed him by his long hair and pulled his head down and kneed him in the face repeatedly, Kahle tried to fight back, punching at J-Money but it didn't do nothing. J-money waited until he knew Kahle was tired and stood him back up and put him in a head lock. Kahle struggled to breathe, he scratched At J-Money arm.

"My brother!" Akoni shouted and tried to run over to him but it was too many henchmen in the way chasing people and shooting darts. He had to stop, aim, and shoot two henchmen in the arm, then dodged behind a tree as darts came flying toward him. Meashell stood right by his side. "We need to get over there. He's killing him." Akoni said.

"We can't make it, it's too many henchmen we need to run while we still can," Meashell said trying to get through to her brother and wanting to just run but couldn't.

A man screaming loud made half the people stop what they was doing, people from the village and the henchmen as J-Money held Kahle in a head lock with one arm, using his biceps to cut of his oxygen, squeezing his neck and with his right hand, he held a hunters knife with riddle edges, and sawed away at Kahle as if he was slicing a turkey for Thanksgiving. Kahle hollered in pain as J-Money sawed away, slicing his neck open and blood squirted out, as his head leaned to the side and he finally stopped screaming. J-Money continued to saw away until Kahle's head was detached and Kahle's body dropped to the sand, blood poured on the sand making it red. J-Money held Kahle's head by his long hair and turned around and lifted it up high for Faith to see.

Faithed smirk her devilish grin and nodded her head in approval.

"No! Nooo!" Akoni shouted and dropped to his knees. "Get up and get to the hut, grab more weapons and head into the jungle, tell everyone to run in the jungle," Meashell said as she ran to the hut and grabbed a short sword made of a bone with tribal marking carved all around it. As flashbacks of Red being pinned to the wall and the conversation she had with Faith about her, saying she almost killed her. Meashell knew what to do, she ran pass a group of henchmen, one jump in front of her, she lifted up his mask and jammed her sword into his eye and pulled it out and kept running.

"She really is a badass, I'm not gonna lie I'm kinda cheering for her," Faith said as she continued to watch Meashell run down on the bitch.

"Listen I don't like the bitch, she crossed me, tried to beat my ass after years of friendship but if that's how we look when we fight. Shit I like watching it too. She's kicking ass but it can't last forever. She's out-numbered and will eventually get tired, any one would. The only way to come out on top in a situation like this is to use your brain, this is chess, not checkers and she's playing checkers hopping around the board with no goal," Jainice said.

As Meashell ran up on J-Money and drop-kicked him in the back with both her feet. J-Money fell forward and dropped Kahle's head as Meashell tried to stab him with the bone sword in the chest. But J-Money rolled to the side before she could. "I forgot how fast you was for a big guy," Meashell said.

"Yea, it's been a while since you trained with me but those good days are gone, you crossed Faith and me," J-Money said popping up off the ground.

"This should be good, Meashell used to train with J-Money a lot," Jainice said.

"Who would win?" Faith asked.

"Most times," J-Money, "One good hit from him and she went down, no matter how skilled we are. A man is a man, but she beat him a few times, she's faster than him, even now. J-Money fast for a man his size, he can't keep up with Meashell." Jainice replied.

"Interesting," Faith said and decided to take a seat at the table Meashell and her family was eating at. She never seen the three little girls crawl from up under it and run into the jungle toward their father.

"I didn't cross no one, y'all delusional. I seen my opportunity for freedom and took it. Shit, you was kidnapped the same night I was, why can't you understand that?" Meashell said while dodging J-Money blows, rolling on the floor popping up and kicking him. "Faith would've let you go free if you asked her. She was following orders from Black Ice to kidnap people, we was supposed to be dead or sold to a third world country but she kept us, taught us new skills and showed us another world that people didn't know existed." J-Money said.

"I wanted none of it, she could have kept it all. I wanted my freedom that's all I cared about J-Money. Yes, she told us she would set us free but when? The slaves was told they'd be set free for years and guess what, we're still slaves with no real rights and get killed by police and they get away with it. Now I got to deal with someone who demands loyalty after taking me from my life, I don't think so," Meashell said while dodging more of J-Money blows.

"You always talk that political stuff but that's not why you being hunted now. Yea when those soldiers came you could've took the opportunity to run and be free but you did more. Which one of you spit on her while she was dying?" J-Money said and front kicked Meashell in the chest, she slid backwards until she fell on her ass and roll backwards then popped back on to her feet in a fighting stance.

"Me and Minglee both spit on that bitch!" Meashell shouted J-Money looked at her as if he wanted to rip her apart with his bare hands. "So not only did you beat her while she was dying, kicking her in the face and chest after they cut her child out of her and shot her then you tried to fight your friend Jainice for trying to help her? You can say what you want, you bitches was fucked up before Faith kidnapped you. The situation just bought out your true nature, you crossed a friend that was like a sister to you, then you beat a bitch when she's down knowing your pussy ass would've never tried it if she was up and moving. You still keep forgetting she came and saved you from the desert room, she didn't put us in there bitch, her father did. He told her to leave us but she refused to listen, you have no loyalty all, that shit you speak is not facts, what's facts and the truth is you're selfish and inconsiderate. Just look at what you done here," J-Money said pointing to the village people fighting and the henchmen over powering them and dragging them away.

"Even if you didn't know that we lived, Faith lived, you know Black Ice is still out there somewhere and would've found you eventually. He never like you, Minglee or Jason, he said that shit in front of all of us, and he still has your friend Tammy. You didn't care about her well-being. What's crazy to me is why you didn't isolate yourself, I would have knowing I'll put anyone close to me in danger and you did just that. That's how you know your character is fucked up. These people had no idea what world you bought them into," J-Money said then laughed. "But you live in this world that only a few know exist, it all shows me that you're not shit Meashell, that you speak that power to the people bullshit, but when it comes down to your life or others you'll put yourself first," J-Money said.

Meashell's facial expression balled up in anger because deep down she knew everything he said was true but the truth hurt. "Fuck you!" Meashell said and spin kicked him then punched him in the face, then stabbed him in the right thigh.

J-Money grabbed his leg, "That shit not gonna work on me." J-Money said as she stabbed him in the left foot with the bone blade. "Ouch! Bitch that stings." J-Money said bending lower to touch his foot.

"I know it won't work, I just needed your talking ass to bend down lower to my thigh, so I can do this." Meashell said and swung with all her might at the side of J-Money's neck, the bone blade rippled edge cut through the muscle, meat, and bone of J-Money's neck, chopping his head clean off.

"Noooooooooo! Nooo!" Faith scream at the top of her lungs, Meashell looked at Faith. Then Faith took off running in her direction.

"Oh shit," Meashell said and ran up the beach and into the jungle.

Faith stopped at J-Money's body and dropped to her knees. "No, no, no this can't be, no, no! Get up my friend, get up please," Faith said then grabbed J-Money's head and tried to put it back on him as if it was a Lego she was building, but it just roll off. She picked his head up again and placed it on her lap and started to cry uncontrollably. "Noo! Noo! I'm so sorry, I'm sorry, you could've left me so many times but you always stood by my side. I'll make that bitch pay I promise."

Jainice and a henchmen walked over to Faith. Faith stood up and passed J-Money head to the henchmen, "Pack this up, he comes with us. Jainice release Egypt and Raven, we're going hunting."

Jainice nodded her head and walked back to the street to a black van and opened the back and Egypt and Raven jumped out and took off. Jainice returned, "What next? No more taking them alive, kill everyone that's left in this village then release the hyenas. We, will leave not one person alive, no bodies. It will look like this village just disappeared in a blink of an eye." Faith sad in an evil voice, as her heart grew colder and darker. She was no longer the person she use to be and could feel lit.

The henchmen pulled out guns and started shooting women and men as they ran, killing them.

A few of the people from the village ran into the jungle as well. Egypt and Raven had a head start, "Release the hyenas," Faith said.

A henchmen backed up an all-black eighteen wheeler truck on the dirt road that led to the village and beach then jungle. He hopped out the truck and looked at the other henchmen loading unconscious peoples bodies into vans. He looked at another henchmen, "I guess she is like her father."

The henchmen looked at him. "No I think she worse, I don't know who scares me more, her or him. Shit I can't remember kidnapping kids; we got children in some of these vans. I heard stories of Black Ice killing a few kids but never kidnapped, now she ordered that everyone left in the village still fighting and running be killed. She's her father's daughter alright and I feel sorry for anyone that crosses her." The other henchmen said.

"Me and you both brother, me and you both." the truck driver henchmen replied as he opened the back of the trailer. Inside it was cages stacked on top of cages. He pressed a button and the cages opened. Hyenas the size of lager dogs leaped out and ran to the beach and to Faith side as she kneeled next to J-Money's body. Faith could feel them there without looking. The henchmen

84

stopped what they was doing and nervously looked at the pack that had to be over twenty five hyenas. They gripped their guns nervously not knowing if the hyenas would attack them. They only seen the animals fear and listen to one person, Black Ice.

Faith stood up without smiling and turned around and the hyenas lowered their heads and sat down, she then turned her head toward the beach where dead bodies lay and people still fighting, then toward the jungle. "Eat!" she said and the hyenas stood up and took off running, splitting into two groups, half went to the beach the other half entered the jungle.

A woman laid on her stomach on the beach shot in the back of her leg, next to her dead friend who was shot in the back of her head. She turned her head to see a baby no older than two, walking lose looking around the chaos of the henchmen killing the villagers. "Come here child, come to me," the woman said. The little boy looked at her while crying, then smiled and started walking, "That's it, cute little baby step closer!" the woman said as the child was only a few more steps away. Then out of nowhere something snatched the child up by his arm and dragged him. Then another one came and grabbed his other arm. The baby screamed and cried as the woman watched in horror as a third hyena came and bit off the child's head in one bite. "Ahh! Nooo!" the woman screamed not believing her eyes as two hyenas ate the child's body in seconds, ripping it to shreds. The woman cried and held her head down then seen the hyena rush to her dead friends body, and started sinking their teeth into her flesh, ripping large chunks of meat and bone away.

The woman could now feeling breathing on the back of her neck, she wanted to scream but didn't. Then a gun shot went off, and whatever was on top of her wasn't anymore. A young man grabbed her hand. "Come, let go, run!" he said with her hand in his right and holding a rifle in his left.

"I can't! I just can't!" the woman cried while hopping with one leg.

"Listen, whatever those things are they are eating everything, even the dead. We can't stay still, you have to keep moving." the young man said as he noticed a group of villagers further down the beach, with tables in front of a hut that they boarded up. "Come, we can make it," the young man said as they ran in the sand and turned around to see henchmen and hyenas chasing them. The young man raised his riffle and squeezed the trigger twice, sent two bullets into a henchmen chest but the bullets bounce right off and didn't slow him down, "Fuck!" he shouted.

"I heard you have to shoot them in the eyes, that's the only way to take them down or take their mask off, or they will keep coming," the woman said while hopping on one leg as fast as she could.

The young man turned around again this time he stopped moving while aiming and squeezed the trigger shooting a henchmen in the eye. "I got one," the young man said raising his arm high in excitement just as a hyena jumped on to his chest knocking him down to the ground and bit his face, he tried to struggle and fight but then felt teeth on his legs and his body being dragged. "Help! Help!" he shouted looking at the lady then at the rifle he dropped.

The woman looked at the hut that wasn't too far away with other people then looked at the young man being dragged back down the beach by two hyenas. "Fuck!" she said thinking of how he just saved her life. She hopped to the riffle and aimed, the sight she saw made her vomit green throw-up onto the sand.

The hyenas was devouring the henchmen body that just got shot, ripping it to pieces and fighting over his body parts. They dragged the young man next to it and started ripping into his stomach pulling his whole stomach out and eating it. "Help me!" the young man cried in pain, looking over his head reaching for the woman.

The woman wiped her mouth with the back of her hand and aimed the rifle and squeezed the trigger, the bullet hit the top of the head of the young man splitting his skull into two, killing him instantly. The hyenas jumped back from the shot and scattered for a second then went back to his body and dragged it further down the beach to eat. The woman turned around and started hopping until she reached the hut, with the other villagers. There was four wooden tables turn over and men shooting rifles at the henchmen and hyenas.

"Come on!" one of them said and the woman recognized him as her brother-in-law Hadrian, "I'm so happy to see you," Hadrian said.

"I don't think we are safe, I think they're gonna kill us all, you got to get more help, I think it so sad, those things just ripped him apart. I seen two of them eat a baby, a baby?" Nani cried.

"We must fight back, a lot of us ran into the jungle but with those things loose I don't think it's a good idea, their like hunting dogs. The smartest thing we can do is make it to the boats and paddle our way off the island to the main island to get help," Hadrian said while firing the rifle.

"That's a good idea, why haven't you done it yet?" Nana asked.

"Because look, at the hut." Hadrian replied while trying not to get distracted because him and six other men continued to fire, sending hails of bullets in the henchmen direction, but it seemed to just slow them down for a second. Nani hopped to the hut, the huts was made of weeds, and look like a beach home, the people in the village used them to store weapons or fishing equipment. Sometimes they'll even sleep in them in the summer time just to feel the ocean breeze.

It was twelve of them running down the beach front line. Nani entered the hut, using the rifle as a cane to see most of the elderly women and men from the village in there. *"Shit no way they can run for the boats before those things grab them or those men; we have to think of something,"* Nani thought to herself. "I got it," she said out loud then hopped back outside to her brother-in-law. "I see the issue, the boats are down the beach, we can see them, but the village elderly are too slow to run for it, what if the men put them down in something like a sleigh and pulled them across the sand," Nani said.

"Hmm that is a good idea but what's gonna keep those things from running up on us or the men from shooting us?" Hadrian replied.

"Fire! We use the coconut tree leaves and make a line, and burn a big fire. They won't be able to cross it and it will give us enough time to reach the boats and paddle away from here." Nani replied.

"That's a good plan, let's do it!" Hadrian said. Him and four men started taking apart the hut using pieces log from it, while the other two men continued firing. Hadrian placed the old women and men on large pieces of flat wood, with rope tied to the end of them.

Nani gathered coco tree leaves and dry bananas leaves and keep her head low while making a perfect straight line across to the hut and to the water. Hadrian grabbed a red can of gasoline and poured it on the leaves then grabbed a torch and set it on fire. Between the dry leaves and gasoline the fires roared and danced.

"Now!" Hadrian said as he and other six men grabbed the ropes and started pulling the elderly down the beach. "Yes, it's working, I knew it would," Nani said while hopping then she looked back to see the henchmen trap by the line of fire, keeping them from crossing.

What happened next made her pee on herself, as the henchmen and hyenas went straight to the ocean and walked through the shallow water to get on the other side, "Oh shit!" Nani shouted. "I didn't think they'd do that! I didn't think they'll do that!" Nani shouted repeatedly.

"What?" Hadrian said looking at Nani hop in front of him.

"They just walked through the water, I didn't think they'd think of that. I thought they'd be stuck looking at the fire until it burned out." Nani shouted as hyenas came and grabbed two old women off the plane that was being dragged on. The four men that was pulling it turned around to grab their rifles off her shoulders to shoot but was too slow as henchmen shot them in the chest and face. They bodies twisted around before they fell dead on the sand, and the hyenas rushed in eating their dead bodies. The screams from the elderly people could be heard as the henchmen shot them in the back or hyenas dragged them away.

"What the hell?" Hadrian said as they made it to the boat, he loaded two boats and Nani got in one, as he tried to load another one the back of his head exploded, he fell face first into the ocean shoreline, the waves hit his body going back and forth.

Nani tried to paddle fast but she was the only strong one in the boat, the old men that was helping was to weak, the waves kept pushing them. Nani looked at the hyenas jump in the water and started swimming, they reached the first boat and snatched the elderly people off and dragged them back to the beach. Nani looked at six hyenas swimming toward her boat. She grabbed the rifle and placed it under her chin and closed her eyes, "God forgive me, but this has to be better than getting eaten alive." Nina thought to herself then pulled the trigger but her arm was yanked, moving the barrel of the gun from up under her chin. Teeth sunk deep into her left arm. "Ahhh!" she screamed as she was pulled into the water. "Ahh!" she tried to scream but water kept getting into her mouth. She could feel her back rest on sand, she coughed up the saltwater, and exhaled deeply just as teeth tore into her chest, eating her breast then lungs. Her body jerked and shook for a second before she died.

Meashell ran deep into the jungle. The jungle in Hawaii was tropical and humid, the temperature changed as they got deeper inside. Big bananas and coconut trees was everywhere and it was easy to get lost but most the villagers hunt and played in jungle most there life. "Meashell! Over here!" Akoni shouted. Meashell spotted them and ran toward him, he was knee low with his wife Laka and his three daughters Kamea, Kaia and Lani. Akoni passed Meashell a high powered hunting bow and a bag full of arrows. "Come, we got to keep moving," he said as the six of them ran deeper into the jungle, they could see other villagers, not too far on the side of them running as well, after running for a good twenty minutes they stopped at a tall tree, you remember this tree as a kid?" Akoni asked.

"Yes, this the one that have the hole in it at the top, we use sleep in it when we ran away." Meashell replied.

"Right! You climb up first then pull the girls up one at a time using the rope, and I'll stand guard," Akoni said holding his rifle. He could hear movement all throughout the jungle mixed with cries for help and laughter. Meashell grabbed the rope and used it to climb up the tree, until she reach the top where there was a big hole in the tree and blankets, she dropped the rope and felt a tug and began to pull it up, she smiled when her oldest niece Kamea reached the top and climbed into the hole. Meashell hugged her then broke their embrace when she heard a bird screeching sound.

Meashell's heart started to beat fast and stomach bubbled, "Oh shit, Raven," she mumbled.

"Listen, I'm gonna climb down, I want you to pull the rope back up as fast as you could, then you don't drop the rope unless you hear your father or mother call for you. Do you hear me?" Meashell said.

"Yes, auntie but," Kamea started to say.

"But nothing, you don't move in here stay perfectly still baby, if anything happens you don't come out that hole not even in the morning, there's a dangerous bird flying around that can see everything, but won't see you if stay still okay," Meashell said.

"Okay auntie." Kamea replied. Meashell knew she didn't have much time, she grabbed the rope and bounced down the tall tree as fast as she could until she reached the ground. She then tugged on the rope and Kamea pulled it up as fast as she could.

"What you doing? Tell Kamea to drop back down the rope for her sisters," Akoni said.

"They will never make it in time up the tree before the wolf gets here! We have to move now!" Meashell said.

"Wolf, we have no wolves in this jungle, and how you know we been spotted?" Akoni asked.

"We have a wolf in it now and hyenas and look up," Meashell said. You see the hawk?"

Akoni looked up to see a large bird about the size of a two-year-old with long wings, it was black and now circling the sky around them. "We don't have hawks here," Akoni look confused.

"We don't have time for this, let's go now1" Meashell said and grabbed Kaia hand and started running. Akoni pick up his daughter Lani into his arms and strapped his rifle on his shoulder and started running while holding on to his wife's' hands. He caught up to Meashell as they ran for their lives, after twenty minutes of straight running they stopped by a river.

"You think Kamea okay?" Lala asked.

"She's safer than us, we got to keep moving," Meashell said.

Akoni was drinking water with his hand from the river. "I blame you for this, you put our family in danger. You put the whole village in danger." Akoni said.

"I told you people might come for me, I warned you. I'm sorry," Meashell said while fighting back tears.

"These aren't people, they chopped our heads off and walk around with it like a trophy and you do the same, you're one of them Meashell. Their demons, not humans, you knew this and knew the problem you bring. Why would you come here and put us all in danger? Yes, you was kidnapped I understand, when I said I'll protect you, it was from people, they're not people, we being hunted by animals and creatures. They took out the whole village and you knew they could do this, why didn't you isolate yourself? You knew we wasn't equipped to handle this Meashell, no one is!" Akoni shouted.

Meashell held her head down knowing he was right, "I didn't think Faith would come for me but I knew in my heart that Black Ice would come for me one day, I should've went with Minglee. Look what I've done to my family." She stopped crying when she heard screeching, "Shit, we been spotted again!" Meashell said.

"How you know?" Akoni asked.

"Every time the hawk screeches, it means it sees us and leads the wolf to us even faster, they hunt together. It's the way Faith trained them. If we hear two sounds from the hawk back to back it mean their right on us and it's too late. We got to move now," Meashell said and grabbed Kaia hand and pulled her and pulled her across the river. Akoni picked up his daughter Lani and followed her.

"We got to get to the mountains, we can lose them there, too many caves to hide in, and ways to the ocean to get off the island," Akoni said. Then they heard screeching back to back, Akoni felt his wife's hand snatched out of his.

"Help! Help!" she screamed. Akoni looked back with his daughter in his arm to see the biggest blackest wolf the color of the night sky. The only reason you could see him clear was because of the night stars and his blue eyes that seemed to glow. The wolf had Laka's left leg in his mouth.

He let go of Laka's calf muscle and stood there growling, looking Akoni in the eyes. Laka fell to the ground and couldn't stand up. "Laka," Akoni said putting down his daughter and taking off his rifle from his shoulder.

"No it's too late, Akoni run!" Meashell yelled.

"I'm not leaving my wife!" Akoni shouted and aimed at Egypt.

"Lani come to me baby, come now," Meashell said knowing they had to keep moving, stopping for too long means something worse will catch up. Lani ran to Meashell.

Akoni aimed his rifle but before he could squeeze the trigger, he let out a loud scream as Raven flew by and scratched his face and kept it moving. Akoni panicked and looked up to the sky while aiming looking for her to attack. He took his eyes off Egypt which was a mistake he regretted.

Egypt had locked on to Laka's leg once more. "Ahhhhh!" she screamed as Egypt dragged her away.

"No no!" Akoni shouted and took off running after her, he aimed and sent two bullets wildly in that direction, but couldn't get a clear shot. The wolf was dragging her through trees and bushes. "Give me back my wife!" Akoni shouted he ran as fast as he could until he seen his wife laying there, he ran over to her to see she was badly bruised from being dragged and lost blood from the bite to her leg, "Baby you okay? Where's did it go! Where is it?" Akoni said bending down, touching his wife's face, and still looking around his environment with his rifle raised.

"It's a trap!" Laka mumbled weakly.

"Huh, what you said?" Akoni asked.

"It's a trap," Laka said then Faith stepped out of the bushes with Egypt by her side. Akoni aimed at her then seen more movements all around him. Hyenas came out of the bushes as well with another young woman.

"So, this her brother, huh?" Faith asked.

"Yea that's him, the only family she got left," Jainice said smiling.

"So you're the one that shot at my Egypt huh" Faith said stepping closer and petting Egypt on the head. Akoni looked around and knew he wasn't going get out this situation alive.

"Listen, we had no idea what Meashell had gotten herself into and I know begging for my life won't help, but I beg you please, don't hurt my children or any of the villages children you find, please." Akoni begged.

Faith walked up to him and kneeled down in front of him so they could be face to face. Akoni looked at her, *"If I attack her, that big ass wolf will eat me and the rest of those creatures will attack. It's something wrong with this woman, she's not normal. I can feel it in my body, it's like she's the devil or just pure evil but there's a little part of her that's good, that still has a soul." Look how she cried when Meashell killed the big guy. You don't have those kind of emotions if you don't love, she loved him, so she has to have a soul? I got to save my daughters."* Akoni thought to himself then looked down at his wife laying on her stomach. "I beg you please let my kids live, I won't fight back," Akoni said and put down the rifle.

"It's sad we had to meet on such circumstances, you have loyalty for your family and village and you're honorable, makes me wonder why these things didn't get installed in Meashell. Did she tell you the full story of how I was gonna let her go anyway and I just needed time so my father would be okay with it. She was never a slave, those fancy moves she used to kill a good friend, she learned because of me. I wanted to make her strong so no one could ever hurt her. Like my father wanted for me, like I'm sure you want for your daughters."

"When I was dying after someone I look at as a mother shot me multiple times and cut my unborn child out of me. Meashell beat me, kicked me and spit on me, instead of trying to help me or pull me out of danger. Now she wants to play the victim. I'm actually sorry I have to do this to your people, but no one can know we exist. Because I like you I'll end it fast, won't let you get eaten alive, that shit look like it really hurts." Faith said as she pulled out a knife and kissed him on the forehead and jammed the knife up under his chin and push it to his brain and yanked it out. She then pulled out her hatchet and started chopping away, until she cut off his head. She picked it up and tossed it to Jainice who put in a bag.

"Ahhhh! Nooooo!" Laka screamed with snot dripping down her nose as she stared at her husband's dead body hit the ground.

Faith turned and looked at her. "Your husband was a very honorable man and for that I'll try not to kill your daughters," Faith looked up at Raven sitting in a tree, then the night sky, "Hunt!" she said and Raven took off and so did Egypt and four henchmen. Faith looked back at Akoni's wife still laying down, "Hunt!" and whispered, "Eat." while her and Jainice walked deep into the jungle.

"Hah hah! Haha!" Laka could hear laughter then looked at the hyenas to see it was them. They rushed Akoni's body and started ripping it to pieces and fighting over body parts. "In less than ten minutes all the skin and meat was picked from his bones and they was now eating the bones up. Laka couldn't stop crying, she held her head down and heard the laugher so close she could feel the hyenas on her skin. She looked up to see Razor's sharp teeth, a hyena bit into the top of her skull, cracking it and ripping it off with some of her forehead and brain. The hyena chewed it like bubble gum as the other hyenas started to devour her, she was dead by the second bite to her face.

Meashell was trying to run faster but Lani kept slowing her down with her little feet, she was six and legs shorter than her other sister Kaia. Meashell looked up and could see Raven and knew they wasn't gonna make it to the mountains without something to slow them down. She stopped running and placed Lani by a short tree. "Lani you have to stay here, auntie will be back for you baby."

"Wait, we gonna leave her? Kaia asked.

"Yes she will be fine," Meashell said lying and grabbed Kaia pulling her with her.

Lani stood there with her hair in two puff pony tails crying. "Don't leave me! Don't leave me!" she cried and could hear something moving in the bushes. Her facial expression ball up in fear as Egypt stepped out. "Auntie! she screamed.

"Why you left her? Why you left my sister?" Kaia screamed and hit Meashell.

"Listen you gonna learn sometimes you have to leave people behind in order for you to keep going, never put no one over yourself. You're the main priority, you can't help no one if you don't help yourself first niece. Now run!" Meashell said.

"You lie! Your lying! My father told you to take care of all of us!" Kaia screamed.

"You know what!" Meashell said and let go of Kaia hand and took off running at full slow speed through the brushes.

"Auntie wait! No don't leave me, Auntie wait!" Kaia said and tried to keep up with Meashell but she was moving too fast. Kaia ran but lost sight of her and didn't know what direction she went. She stopped running looking for any sign of her. "Auntie! Auntie please don't let them get me. Auntie!" Kaia said with tears in her voice and could hear laughter. Kaia ran not knowing where she was going but doing her best to get away from the laughter, she tripped and fell face first into some mud, then heard laughter all around her. "Auntie! Auntie! Help please," Kaia cried as the hyenas came out from behind trees and bushes and moved in close to her. "Auntie!" was her last word.

"Shit, I hope that bought me more time. I can't let them close in on me, once I get in the tunnels of the mountains I can get to the other side and find a boat, then get off this island and link up with Minglee. I should of just went with her in the first place but I now regret I didn't." Meashell thought to herself as she made it to the mountains, she smiled while climbing on it, walking sideways, and finding the pathway to climb up, it took her ten minutes before she found entryway, she entered and could see lights up a head from a torch. She ran toward it to see two men and three women from the village.

"You scared us, I thought you was one of them," one of the men said.

"Fabio, I remember you, no, but we got to keep moving. How long before we get to the other side of the mountain, I haven't been in here since I was a kid?" Meashell asked.

"It's gonna take a while, where's your brother and his wife?" Fabio asked.

"I'm sorry to say but those people got him and they're gonna get us too if we don't get to the damn ocean and out of here," Meashell said taking a torch out the hands of one of the other men and started power walking. The mountain tunnel was dark and wet, and were longer before anyone in the village could remember, but every villager and child played in the, or walked to the other side to get to the best fishing spots.

"Meashell! Meashell! Why are you running! Face me!" Meashell heard Faith's voice echo through the tunnels.

"Oh fuck no!" Meashell said and start running.

Fabio, the two women and guy that was with him followed her lead. The sound of laughter echoed in the cave, Fabio looked back to see hyenas chasing them. One if the women screamed as a hyena jumped on her back and knocked her to the ground and four more surrounded her. One ripped out her throat before she could scream again.

The second woman stopped for a second to catch her breath. She looked up and Fabio and the men she was with was gone, she stood up.

"Fabio!" she called out in fear, then turned around and heard growling. She turned around to see a pair of beautiful blue eyes staring at her and a pair of little reds eyes. The woman waited until her eyes adjusted to the dark and urinated on herself, hot piss dripped down her right leg as a tall black wolf stepped out of the darkness, and sitting on his back was a bird the size of a two-year-old child. "Please no! Stay, don't come closer," the woman said while steeping backwards.

The bird took off flying, the woman couldn't even see it because she was so fast as she ripped off the woman nose. "Ahh!" the woman screamed holding her nose and screamed falling on the ground. She stood back up and ran, holding what was left of her nose as her blood dripped down her face on to the ground. She stopped and noticed it was three tunnels to pick from, she took her hand and run the back of it on the tunnel in the middle then the left and ran down the right tunnel, knowing the wolf and bird was probably tracking her blood.

Egypt and Raven stopped when they reached the three tunnel, and sniffed the air, the woman's blood was fresh and smelled sweet, they started to go down the left tunnel but stopped, they could hear her footsteps as she ran and heavy breathing. They followed their instincts and they ran down the right tunnel, the woman stop for a second and leaned on the wall to catch her breath, "I guess I need to stop smoking so much hookah," she said out loud to herself. While bending down looking at her feet, she looked up and she was face to face with those beautiful glowing blue eyes, it was the last thing she seen as Egypt locked onto her neck, breaking it, killing her instantly and started to rip her apart with Raven. They ate her together like Faith had taught them.

Meashell could still hear Faith's voice calling out to her and the hyenas footsteps gaining on them. "We're not going to outrun them," Meashell said and looked at the man running with Fabio, she slowed down then hit him in the head with the torch, he stumbled backwards.

"What you doing?" he groaned in pain. Meashell placed the torch to his clothes then set him on fire. "Ahhh! Ahh!" he screamed while patting his shirt.

Meashell smiled and ran, Fabio went back to help him, "Drop to the floor and roll, roll!" Fabio shouted. The man dropped to the ground and rolled as his hair caught fire. Fabio continued to pat the man even though the fire was burning his hand, he stopped when he looked up to see seven hyenas. "I'm sorry," Fabio said and started running.

"Wait don't leave me, don't leave me," the man said as he rolled a few more times and was finally able to put out the fire, he sat up in pain. Then cried when he heard growling mixed with laughter. He stopped crying and started laughing "hah hah hah ha!" his laughter echoed throughout the tunnel, the hyenas looked at him crazy. One stepped closer then locked on to his jaw and mouth. He started to scream, his screams and the smell of his blood excited them as the hyenas ripped off his jaw and the others attacked as if they hadn't eaten seven people already for the night.

"No!" he cried as one bit off his hand and another bit into his thigh running off with a chunk of his flesh. "No," he tried to say as another rushed to his stomach and started chewing real fast until his stomach bust open. This excited the hyenas more. The man wondered how he was still alive, he could feel every bite and tug. The pain was more than he could bare, tears streamed down his face as another hyena bit into his chest. He could then feel one bite through his boot until he snatched off his foot. "Ughh!" he groaned in pain, half his face was eaten. He moved around weakly and could hear footsteps, he looked to see a dark-skin woman looking down at him as she slowly walked by, he reached out with what was left of his arm to her, for help just to have a hyena bite his arm off and run off into a corner with it as another one came and tried to take it from him. He decided to close his eyes as a hyena locked it's teeth on to his heart and ripped it out.

"What's wrong with you? Why would you do that? He was one of us! We don't hurt our kind, have the outside world change you so much, made you so cold?" Fabio said while running behind Meashell. Their tribe never turned against one another, they believe in peace but be warriors to the outside world, never harm a brother or member of the tribe. Feed each other, eat with one another, keep these rules no matter how things change with society and technology, to still keep parts of their old ways.

Meashell took the bow that was around her shoulders and an arrow and turned around and aimed at Fabio. No, the outside world didn't do this to me, I learned you have to put yourself first," Meashell said while aiming.

"That's a lonely way to live." Fabio said and stopped running.

"Yes, but I'll still be alive," Meashell said and shot the arrow. Fabio moved in time and tried to rush her. Meashell pulled out another arrow and shot him in the leg, Fabio dropped to the ground but used the wall to get back up.

"Your brother welcomed you back home, we all did. You was a sister, daughter, aunt, cousin to us all," Fabio said.

"Not really, I remember y'all use to tease me about my dark-skin complexion, laughed at me because I was only half Hawaiian, called me African booty scratcher. I remember all those hurtful things." Meashell said.

"We was kids, children don't know better but you was always accepted and loved," Fabio said.

"Yea, by my father and brother, the rest of y'all looked at me as if I was an outsider and didn't belong, scared I was gonna bring more dark babies into the village. I was never brown enough so to be real, fuck y'all," Meashell said.

"We can outrun them together, it don't have to be like this." Fabio replied.

"I don't have to outrun them, I just have to outrun you," Meashell said and shot Fabio in the thigh and took off running again. Fabio pulled one of the arrows out that hit his lower leg and looked at the one in his thigh and got scared, knowing it could've hit the major artery, if he pulled it out he could bleed to death. He could hear foot steps behind him, he leaned on the wall and turned around, to see a beautiful dark-skin woman with hair that stopped at her shoulders.

"She did this to you huh?" Faith said while smiling.

Fabio tried to stand up straight so he could die with pride. "Yes," he groaned in pain.

Faith chuckled, "That bitch something else, she kinda ruthless, in a another lifetime we would have been great friends but I'm to loyal and couldn't do half the shit she does. She really don't give a fuck about no one." Faith said thinking out loud then looked at Fabio. "If it's any consolation know she will suffer; now you have two options, I'm not gonna kill you myself, I feel bad for you. You can pull that arrow out your leg, that I'm sure hit your artery, you know it as well that's why you didn't pull it out." Faith said looking at the other arrow on the floor, "Or you could wait until the hyenas finish eating your friend back there, which won't be long, they're greedy animals, they eat fast and don't stop even when they're full. They'll walk around with pot belly's looking pregnant. I don't know how they do it. Any time I eat that much I'm ready to sleep and start to move slow, but to each its own." Faith said as she continued walking as if she didn't have a care in the world.

Fabio looked at her, then the arrow on the floor, *"Should I try to kill that bitch, stick the arrow in her back? Something not right with her but she killed so many of my people, my friends, my son, they took a lot of them as well, fuck it."* Fabio thought to himself and picked up the arrow on the floor and hopped as fast as he could with the arrow raised high and jammed it into the back of Faith's head. She fell face first, he hopped back then hopped over her body. "That's for my people bitch."

Faith reached back and pulled the arrow out and slowly stood up. "Every time I try to be nice and show people mercy y'all show me why I shouldn't." Faith said looking at the bloody arrow.

"But how?" Fabio said, and his mind screamed, pull it out. Pull it out." He reached for the arrow in his leg but Faith was already up on him and punched him in the face then knocked his hand away, she then bent down and broke the arrow in his leg from the front and back, bending the thick wood inside him. "There, now the only way to get that out is to cut it out," Faith said and punched him in the stomach. "I felt bad for you, I dropped my guard and wanted to see what you would do, what choice you'd pick. You could've ran, that would have been smart, or pulled the arrow out your leg and died peacefully. But you chose to stab the devil in the back," Faith said while laughing.

Her laugh sent chills down Fabio's spine and he seen her for the first time for what she really was, what she's been hiding. He dropped to his knees and started praying, he opened his eyes to see he was surrounded by hyenas and a very large wolf with blue eyes. Behind them was more of those men that dressed in all black with black mask holding guns. "If this how I go Lord know I tried." Fabio mumbled while crying. He open his eyes again and the wolf and hyenas was gone. Faith was kneeled down face to face with him. "What are you?" Fabio asked as his body trembled.

Faith kicked him in the head. "You taught me a lesson today, you don't die here today sir, you'll be with me a long time, so I can never forget that lesson, when I do start to forget it, I'll look at you and remember."

"Huh?" Fabio said confused.

"And I'm the daughter of the devil," Faith said and squeezed the trigger. Fabio felt something hit him in the chest, it hurt and felt like a bee sting, he looked down to see Faith holding a dart gun and a dart now in his chest before he lost consciousness. Faith stood up and looked at the henchmen. "Load him up with my personals," Faith said. Cricket looked at the other henchmen and they grabbed Fabio's body and dragged him out the caves.

Meashell could see the exit of the tunnel. Out the other side was a beautiful view and boats. She smiled as she exited the cave and smelled the night air, she looked up to the sky and then looked on the beach and her heart dropped. Jainice was waiting at the beach with ten henchmen and two hyenas. "Meashell! Meashell," Faith said over and over in a soft voice and it echoed through the tunnel.

"Shit! Shit, okay think fast, go back in the caves and face Faith and her wolf, or take on Jainice and the henchmen, I can kill the henchmen but Jainice would take time, maybe I just need enough time to get into one of those boats with an engine." Meashell thought to herself. "Fuck it!" she said and walked toward the beach with the bow and arrow in her hand. She aimed and shot one of the hyenas in the head, it dropped to the sand and died instantly. She aimed at the next one and shot it in the chest.

"You only gonna piss her off more by killing the pets," Jainice said.

"Fuck you! You think I care if I piss that psycho bitch off," Meashell said.

"You should." Jainice replied.

"It was you! You told her about this place? You and Minglee was the only ones that knew about this side of my family," Meashell said.

"Yep and remember the story you told me about the mountain and caves, that's how I knew your ass would be here." Jainice responded.

"Jainice what are you doing? We was friends, you was like a big sister to me, why are you fighting for this bitch? Run with me, we can go somewhere where she can't find us, you don't have to be loyal to her," Meashell said.

"Shit,

"I see how you treat your friends and family and you killed one of my friends, I really didn't know how fuck up of an individual you was until tonight. I guess the signs was always there but we paint pictures of people on how we want to see them or want them to be, the potential in them, more than what they actually are. I wouldn't run down the block with you, yet alone cross Faith. I'm sure J-Money told you, we was free, we're free now, we're not her slaves, the henchmen aren't her slaves, they're here because they want to be, so am I. I have enough money in overseas account to go anywhere in the world I want to and live the life I want but I chose to be with here, you should've did the same." Jainice replied.

"You sound fucking stupid, the bitch kidnapped me, trained me to kill and not expect me to try to kill her." Meashell replied.

"Let me ask you to think, since you want to be so slow. Let's speak facts before I kill you. One, you did know her father made her kidnap people and we was one of her first right?" Jainice asked.

"Yes, so." Meashell replied.

"Bear with me, I want to make sure you get it. Two, she decided not to listen to her father. God knows we all fucking scared of him. If the man told any one of us to jump right now, we all would be trying to jump high enough to reach the moon so he don't get upset and put our body parts in jars right?" Jainice said.

"Yea, what's your point?" Meashell said.

"So she defied her father, the scariest man on this earth and put her life in danger to save us from the feeding room, then trained us and promised to let us all free as soon as her father's eyes wasn't on us right?" Jainice asked.

"So, we wouldn't have been there in the first place if it wasn't for her." Meashell said.

"Did she ever mistreat you, did she treat you like a sister, the only time she was hard on us was during training and it was easy to see why with all the henchmen being men and all and the way her father was hard on her when it came to fighting?" Jainice asked.

"What's your point, I never wanted none of this and never wanted to be there, so fuck her!" Meashell shouted.

"Well, fuck you too!" Meashell heard Faith say from behind her, she turned around to see Faith with her wolf by her side and her hawk on her arm.

Meashell looked back at Jainice, "All that talking, you was just killing time until she got here huh," Meashell said.

"Mostly, but I was making a point." Jainice replied.

"I don't know how y'all here right now, y'all supposed to be dead. I watched the building collapse on y'all. I'll kill you just like I killed J-Money," Meashell said pointing the arrow at Faith head.

"Yes, you killed a very close friend to us and you're gonna pay for that, pay for spitting on me while I was dying," Faith said.

"Get on with it then bitch," Meashell said.

"Oh no, I'll get to you soon enough. I promised Jainice I'll let her whip your ass, you was her friend in another lifetime and you and Minglee jumped her and left her for dead. I know how I feel and only knew you for two years, she knew you longer, so that pain got to run deeper," Faith said.

"Fuck you!" Meashell said and moved from pointing at Faith to pointing the arrow at Raven and released the arrow and it spun through the air.

A flashback of when she first started training played in Faith's mind, how a henchmen threw knives at her and she kept missing them, Black Ice would yell and say, "Use your mind, then your hands, see where it's going and be there." Faith's heart raced knowing if she messed up Raven would be dead. Faith focused and caught the arrow just in time.

Meashell loaded another arrow and shot again. This time she hit Egypt's front leg. "You bitch!" Faith said as Raven took off flying. Faith spin kicked Meashell knocking the bow and arrow out of Meashell's hand, then black flipped and kicked Meashell in the chin.

"Fuck, I'm not gonna be able to beat this crazy hoe, she been fighting longer than me and trained by her father. I just need to buy time to reach one of those boats," Meashell thought to herself, as

Faith sent blow after blow toward her. Meashell blocked a few of her punches and punched back but Faith was too fast and seemed like the madder she got the faster she was.

"You shot Egypt and you killed J-Money," Faith said while trying to grab her but Meashell kept knocking her hands down and managed to land a punch to the chest, she soon kicked at Faith but Faith caught her leg in mid-air and used her elbow to keep hitting Meashell's thigh.

"Ahh! Ahh!" Meashell screamed trying to break her leg free as Faith continued to drive her elbow into Meashell. Meashell leaned down and grabbed a handful of sand and tossed it at Faith's face. Sand went all into her eyes and mouth making her release Meashell's leg.

Meashell rubbed her thigh and squeezed it, to make the pain stop. It felt as if she had a charlie-horse, she tried to stand on it and put pressure on to her leg but couldn't, she rubbed it and tried again. "That's better," she looked at Faith still spitting out sand and rubbing her eyes. Meashell smiled and attacked, kicking Faith in the face. "Does that feel familiar bitch!" Meashell shouted then punched Faith in the ribs five times. "How about this?" Meashell shouted. "I was happy when I seen you bleeding to death that day, and you think I was going to miss the opportunity to kick you when you was down , I'll do it again! I don't regret nothing," Meashell said while grabbing Faith hair and punched her in the face.

Jainice was about to move in but saw Faith raising her hand to tell her, "Wait don't." Jainice stopped. "How did she know, can she see right now if so why she letting Meashell beat her ass." Jainice said to herself and stood back and watched.

"Fuck you! Fuck your daddy, fuck your wolf, your damn bird and fuck that baby of yours!" Meashell said then swung. Faith caught her fist and squeezed, "Ahhhh!" Meashell screamed as Faith broke free from the grip she had on her head.

"My father said never really let someone know how strong I really am. Guess he was right." Faith said and looked down at Meashell now on her knees, Meashell tried to pull her hands free but couldn't, she tried hitting her.

"How is she doing this?" Meashell cried as Faith squeezed tighter and tighter. "Ahhhhhh!" Meashell hollered.

"This for saying fuck my baby," Faith said and you could hear the bones in Meashell's hand breaking. Faith let her go and spin kicked her in the face, Meashell hit the sand and looked at her right hand, "What did you do? What are you?" Meashell shouted.

"You're a fucked up person and another life lesson I needed to learn, you looked so sweet and so innocent then boom! Evil selfish bitch!" Faith said and walked over to Egypt and pulled the arrow out her leg, "Don't worry baby, you'll get fixed up," Faith said while rubbing her head.

Meashell popped up and took off running while holding her hand, she ran down the beach to the docks and could see the boat, she jumped on one and pulled the cord so it could start but nothing happen she pulled it again and still nothing, "No! No!" Meashell shouted as Jainice walked to her slowly with henchmen by her side. "No! No!" Meashell screamed as two henchmen ran up on her and pulled her out the boat. She tried to fight but couldn't because of her hand, they pushed her head down in the water and held it there, lifting her up and then pushing back under.

"Bring her in," Jainice said, then the henchmen lifted Meashell head out the water and walked her back to the beach. Meashell coughed up saltwater and rolled over onto her back.

"I'm disappointed, one, I was hoping to fight you but it's not gonna be fair with your hand broken and two, I thought you'll put up a better fight than this , shit I thought we would need way more men catching you." Jainice said looking down at her.

"Fuck you bitch! I know you did this to me. She would've never known about all of this. I swear I'm gonna kill you one day I swear!" Meashell shouted.

"'No you're not," Jainice said kicking Meashell in the head then shot her in the face with a dart before Meashell could scream she lost consciousness.

Chapter 5

Faith sat on the back porch looking at the night sky. Jainice walked out the back door. "You good?" Jainice asked.

"No, I'm still hurting over losing J-Money, but the Texas air helps. I like it here for some reason, it helps relaxing me, it's better than staying on those compound bases. To be real I've never stayed in a house this big." Faith replied.

"Yea, I like this house too and the fact it's a secret elevator to a small compound base downstairs is pretty cool." Jainice replied.

"Yea it is," Faith said.

"I feel you on losing J-Money, I cried for two days but if I stop thinking about it I'll be okay." Jainice said.

"You're right and it looks like it's late enough for me to take Egypt for a walk without the neighbors seeing or freaking out." Faith said.

"Shit at night, you just look like some rich bitch in this neighborhood walking a Great Dane dog, I once seen a woman walk one and got close to me, at that time it was the scariest thing I saw. Funny to think of it now but I didn't know if I wanted to run or stand there and watch it." Jainice said.

"What did you do?" Faith asked.

"I stood the fuck still and watched the damn big dog pass me. I'm not stupid and things that scare us is sometimes beautiful, like when your killing people, I know they be scared but they get to see the real you for just a second before they die." Jainice said.

"See you been smoking too much again, every time you do, you get all deep and shit. You got another blunt?" Faith said laughing.

"Yea," Jainice pulled one out her pocket and sat next to Faith, they stared at the water in the pool as Jainice lit the blunt, "So what's next? You gonna have to start running shit more, you got Lefty doing everything. I know his head is killing him, I got him smoking weed now and you know he never touches it," Jainice said, then passed the blunt to Faith.

"Yea, I'll run things soon enough, but right now I need to find that bitch and her husband to get my baby back. I keep thinking that getting Jason and Meashell felt good but it's still don't stop the pain I'm in. I won't be complete until I find my child," Faith said fighting back her tears.

"We will find them, one thing for sure Black Ice built something big with this organization so a henchmen, a camera system, something or someone is gonna to spot them." Jainice said.

"What if the bitch change her face again? I got everyone watching the Dominican Republic, shit I didn't even know it was Sabrina with the face job they did to her and the bitch could act. I really thought she was an old lady," Faith said giggling then pass the blunt.

"Yea, me too. That bitch really had me thinking she was an old lady but I never liked her, it was something about her eyes. I use to swear she was spitting in your food while cooking it," Jainice said.

"Yea, now I'm thinking of it, she could have. My dumb ass had her cooking me breakfast and dinner, the bitch can cook. I guess good cooking don't keep a man because he still cheated on her and I'm still not sure why she is more mad at me than her husband. None of this would've ever happened if he didn't fuck me and lie to me, shit I wouldn't even be who I am now," Faith said.

"See the weed getting to you too." Jainice replied and passed the blunt, "But women never really get mad at the men, some do but take them back anyway, it's easier for them to blame the women, saying she wants my man. Naw, bitch your man wants me or her and starts telling lies, spitting that game, and throwing money then put down some good dick without mentioning he's married or in a relationship. Shit always happens like that but I guess their working together because you killed their children even their dog, at the time you didn't know how that affected them because you never had nothing you love or anyone for that matter. Now look at you, how you feel from the lost of J-Money? Or when Egypt got shot three days ago, how did that make you feel?" Or better yet when they took your child?" Jainice said while exhaling deeply and blowing out smoke.

Faith sat there thinking about what Jainice said. *"She's right, I didn't know the feeling of lost until now. I wasn't wrong for killing Antonio's sons, they tried to rape me but I was wrong for killing their daughter. I was lost in rage, blind by it, shit if they feel the same pain I'm feeling for the loss of my child, I can understand why they went so hard to get revenge but fuck that they still got to pay."*

"Here take this," Jainice said.

"Huh, what happened?" Faith replied.

"Bitch, I been trying to pass you this blunt for ten minutes now your ass been stuck, just staring straight at the pool, high as hell," Jainice said.

"I wasn't talking?" Faith asked.

"Hell no, maybe in your head." Jainice said causing them both to start laughing.

"I got to stop smoking, your weed be too damn strong I be day dreaming and shit but I was saying Antonio and Sabrina have every right to feel the way they do and I understand their pain but fuck that, they pulled me into that shit. That bitch knew about me and called me a cheap hoe. They both tried to give me to their sons and their friends, they thought their money made them better than people. Superior and I was just trash. Once I find those two and Minglee ass, I can't forget her, I'll never forget the feeling of her kicking me in the head as I died and she spitting in my face. That shit plays over and over in my head. Does that happen to you?" Faith asked.

"Yea, I dream of it sometimes, I was scared not going to lie to you but you said trust you, I did. I just thought we was going to go to hell together." Jainice replied.

"What hell? You think we going to hell when we die?" Faith asked while smiling and getting up.

"Bitch yes, we not going to the other place but if and when we end up in hell, we will run the motherfucking place," Jainice said getting up as well.

"I'm done with your ass for the night, grab my hatchet off the dining room table and gun and tell Cricket to bring Egypt and Raven to me. I'm going for a walk, the night sky is beautiful out here and clear, and after that blunt I need to walk it off and eat," Faith said and Jainice step into the house and came back out.

"I don't know why you feel the need to carry all of this in this bougie ass neighborhood, Egypt is more than enough to scare anyone around her in sugarland." Jainice said.

"Shit, don't sleep on Texas; Texas is hood no matter how pretty the houses are or big and my father said it's better to have my weapons and don't need them and to need them and don't have it." Faith replied and put the hatchet in the holster on her back and her gun on her side holster, as Cricket came out with a leash and Egypt close to him and Raven flew out the back door into the night sky.

"What if she eats someone's kid?" Cricket asked. "There's no children out this late, she's good. Have everyone gone as I planned?" Faith asked.

"Yea Mistress, we sold all the Hawaiians from that village and followed orders and kept all the children, no harm came to them and their training will start soon. They're at the compound base in Northern California and I keep the other two for us, they will train with me and other henchmen and kept close as you ordered." Cricket replied.

"Good there's a lot about my father's organization I don't know, no one knows. That's what we have to figure out and we need to find him but now's not the time to discuss this," Faith said and was about to walk off with Egypt by her side.

"Mistress wait, you forgot something," Cricket said handing her a remote the size of a car key.

"I don't need this." Faith responded.

"Not for nothing, we don't know if Antonio will attack again, remember he has a mercenary army at his disposal, we don't know if they're looking for us like we looking for them, you press this button, and the fourteenth henchmen that on this basement will come running, and others will come from the compound base not far from here. I let you down before I won't let you down again," Cricket said meaning every word.

Faith took the remote with the big red button and touched Cricket's face gently, she didn't allow none of the henchmen to wear masks at this location so they could blend in. "You didn't fail me Cricket, you was following orders that day, you got the vehicle like you was told, you thought you left me with henchmen and you did J-Money and Jainice and we didn't know who Ella-Ana was at the time so don't blame yourself I don't. What matters to me is that you came back for me. That you and Lefty didn't stop until you found my body, if y'all didn't do that I would have been buried down there forever. I love you and know you have my back my friend, so don't worry. Make me proud, keep me safe and find that bitch Sabrina for me. Now, let me go before you blow my high," Faith said and got on her tiptoes and kissed him on the forehead, then turned around and walked off with Egypt by her side. She looked down at her smartwatch that counted her steps, okay we gonna do about five-thousand steps tonight and don't rush me girl; I just like to look at things while we walk. Faith said and Egypt looked at her funny."

"Whatever," Faith said then pet Egypt on the head, as they walked their normal routine.

Faith looked up and could see Raven flying, it seems like she grows more and more every day, she was big enough now to pick a dog or a child up easy and take them with her. Some of the neighbors had dogs but when they smelled Egypt they wouldn't bark at all. "Not for nothing Egypt I like it here, I've never been to a neighborhood like this, shit I like Texas. I think I want to make this our permanent base, but father would always say don't get comfortable and he was right, the last time I did someone took my baby but a place like this would be perfect for a child, the homes got pools, it's a family friendly neighborhood."

"This the stuff people dream of, I dream of, I can walk you at night and no one notices you're a wolf not a dog and if they do what I'll say is you're one of those Alaskan huskies, or better yet I'll buy land and you can run around it so we don't have to keep moving state to state. I just want to be in one place with my family and friends, I think that's all I wanted. I want to hear something even more crazier, I miss my damn father, he's an asshole and the devil but he loves me and it's weird that he been missing this long, unlike him, think after I kill that bitch and her husband I'll start looking for him. Something in my stomach says he's in trouble." Faith said to Egypt as Egypt stopped and sniffed a tree, they'd been walking for a good twenty minutes.

Faith looked at her watch to see how many steps they got in. "I have questions I'm high, so I got two legs and got 2,000 steps in so far and you got four legs does that mean you got 4,000 steps in cause of your extra legs. This a question I got to ask Jainice next time we smoke. The weed be having me thinking of crazy shit like that," Faith said then felt a chill down her back, as if someone had taken a fan and put it up her shirt. It was a feeling she felt when her father was around and was told it was the same feeling other people get from her as well. Kinda like fear mixed with the feeling to run, as if your body was talking to you.

"Father," Faith said looking around up and down the block. But didn't see nothing then Egypt started growling in a low tone up the block. Faith looked in the direction Egypt was growling up the block, six houses up on the corner was a little boy standing in the shadows, he had to be no older than ten or eleven. Next to him with a shadow of a dog taller than him. Faith tried to see them clearly but couldn't, it was as if they blended in with the dark and all you could make out was their silhouette.

Faith squinted her eyes, "Why the fuck is that boy just standing there looking at us, and his dog is as big as you Egypt but wider or fatter I can't tell." Faith said then looked down at Egypt when she looked back up the boy was gone. "I must've smoked too much weed or there has to be something in it. I'm tripping tonight, what they call this...anxiety. Well, my anxiety acting the fuck up," Faith said then Egypt turned around and started growling low to warn her. Faith turned around fast and could see the same boy now across the street. Now the boy stood in the shadows again with his dog, just standing there looking at her without moving an inch. The same creepy chill traveled up her spine, the one her father gave her and the feeling she gave other people. "What the fuck is this?" Faith then whistled so low that only dogs and birds could hear it.

Raven flew to her as she stretched out her arm, she landed on it. Faith continued to look at the boy not taking her eyes off him this time. "Watch," Faith said as her and Raven watched the boy, Raven took off into the night sky blending in with her dark feathers of midnight and let out a screech. Faith pulled out one of her hatchets. Then a man stood next to the boy, they both just stood there staring from the shadows. The man was big 6'1 tall and from his silhouette he was muscular and wide, kinda built like Black Ice but shorter. Faith knew it wasn't her father. "One he is too wide but has my father shoulders. But he also doesn't have Black Ice's signature trench coat and that man loves his trench coat leather or cotton," Faith said to herself.

Everyone in the world has energy her father taught her. *"You can feel most peoples energy right away, they can't hide it. If their liars, good people, or bad people, you'll be able to feel it right away, if someone is a piece of shit, only a few people can hide it, those good liars that lie so good they actually believe it themselves even when they know it's not true, but animals can always feel it."* Black Ice's words played in her mind and the energy she was feeling off these two was wrong, it was dark and evil but not quite like her father or hers. The man and the boy with his dog stepped to the side and Faith could no longer see them; she looked up and Raven lost track of them as well or she would've screeched pin-pointing their location.

"What the fuck is going on here." Faith bent down while keeping her eyes on the corner and took off Egypt's leash and started walking toward the corner, and Egypt started whimpering. Faith looked down at her, "Girl, don't be scared, we doing the scaring out here, they don't scare us. We're the thing that goes bump at night, you know the most deadly thing in the world is a woman. All the real hunters are females, lions, wolves, dogs, and humans. We just let men think their strong because their weak egos can't take it. They'll be crying ducks, they will never be hard they'll look for a weak or younger female because they're scared of alpha woman. That's what me and you are, alpha women, now don't forget that." Faith said then bent down and kissed Egypt on the nose. She stood up and walked around the corner of the block.

Raven made a screeching sound and Faith looked up to see where she was, she was five houses down, circling a beautiful two-story brick home. Faith put her hatchet back in her holster and started to walk toward the home. Once she passed three homes, the same chill sensation traveled down her back. She could see the little boy standing in the doorway, but still couldn't see his face. Inside the house was pitch black, he continued to stare at Faith as she moved closer and closer to the house. Once she was one house away, he stepped backwards into the house and disappeared with the darkness. "I don't know what's up with this kid but I've never been scared of the dark, I always felt like it was home, shit we are the things that come out the dark," Faith said.

"I don't know why but I just need to ask that boy a question," Faith said and looked behind her. She could see Jainice duck behind a car, a block away acting as if she wasn't following her. *That girl really need to work on her sneaking up on people skills for real, she look like a damn five-year-old playing tagged and hiding behind a skinny ass pole, talking about do you see me.* Faith thought to herself then continued to the house. She stood in front of it, studying it. The door was wide open. Egypt looked at her. "Well, we can't stay out here forever, it looks like they want us to come in Egypt, I'm curious to see what all of this about, I got butterflies in my stomach. Let's do this," Faith said as she walked up the stairs to the front door and stepped in and Egypt was right behind her.

A loud slam could be heard as the front door shut behind them and locked. "Oh that was dramatic as hell," Faith said out loud.

"I'm here! Come out and talk! What's with all the creepy hiding in shadows and disappearing? It's a neat trick but I don't have time for tricks or games, I get bored easily and got more pressing concerns to worry about. So what's up!

"So, he didn't teach you the shadow trick huh?" Faith heard a man say in a deep voice.

Faith looked around the whole house, it was empty as if no one lived there. She walked into the living room, a little bit of light from the moon shine through the house's glass backdoor that led to the pool area. The house was designed just like Faith's. The only difference between the two homes is that Faith had a secret elevator that led to hold base that took up four homes, where her henchmen stay and a few people she kidnapped. A man stepped out the dark and in to the living room, in one hand he gripped a chrome machete that looked a lot like Black Ice's but his had rippled edges, in his right hand he held a very large chrome gun, a .50 caliber Desert Eagle. *This guy likes chrome a lot I see.* Faith thought to herself. She studied him up and down, he looked almost like her father, but his face wasn't all the way there and his eyes was cold but not cold enough, his body was shaped like Black Ice's maybe even a little stronger. "You ready?" he asked.

"I don't even know what this is, who are you and where's the little boy?" Faith replied.

"I asked are you ready?" the man said again.

"Ready for what?" Faith asked with her facial expression twisted up, wondering what the fuck he was talking about.

"To die," the man said and raised the chrome .50 caliber handgun and squeezed the trigger without hesitation.

"What the fuck!" Faith shouted and pulled out one of her hatchets and raised it to her face. The bullet hit it, the impact from it pushed her back, making her feet slide, but the bullet bounced off the hatchet and hit the floor.

"Hmmm neat trick, what's your blade made of?" the man said calmly.

"Fuck you," Faith said and pulled out her Glock 26 and fired two rounds at him. He moved in the shadows and dodged the bullets. Egypt slowly crept in to the dark, waiting for Faith tell her it was her opportunity to attack. "Don't hide in the dark pussy, the dark don't scare me and you don't either, you shot at me, now come out and face the consequences like a man," Faith said.

"Sure," the man said and came out firing sending three bullets in Faith's direction she side flipped then back flipped moving out the way.

"Four more," Faith mumbled to herself, counting his bullets and she fired back, missing him. *"For a big guy he moves fucking fast but I'm not about to be shooting at this floor all night.* Faith thought to herself and looked behind her at the first door.

"There's no way out and your men won't be coming to get you, we soundproofed the house, you can shoot or scream and no one will hear. It's your time to die," the man said.

"Fuck this shit." Faith put her gun back in the holster and ran straight at him, he fired four times then dropped his gun when he noticed he didn't hit Faith at all. Faith jumped up in the air and swung, hitting him in the face with her left fist. He backstepped and touched his chin.

"You're stronger than you look."

"Hmmm, you have no idea," Faith said as he swung the machete trying to slice her in half, she stepped to the side just in time. He continued to attack her with anger as if she stole something from him, swinging the machete at her face then chest then legs, "Fuck he fast," Faith said out loud then started blocking his blows with her hatchet. When the metal from her hatchet and his machete hit , speaks of orange lit up the dark room, each time Faith could see the little boy in the dark from the corner of her eyes, just watching, one time he was in the dining room and the next time he was in the kitchen, each time he was never in the same spot but always just standing and looking. *That little nigga creepy as hell. I don't give a fuck, he belongs in a horror move. I thought I was scary, and they both move to fast. Who the hell are they and why does he want me dead?" Did Antonio and Sabrina send them, more mercenaries or professional killers, he's definitely a killer, look at how he swings the machete."* Faith thought to herself, then punched him in the mouth twice and front kicked him in the chest and swung low trying to chop his leg off. He raised his leg just in time for the hatchet to miss him, then looked at his gun on the floor. Faith watched where his eyes went, "Pussy scared to make it a fair fight huh," Faith said.

"This isn't a game," the man said and spin kicked, hitting her in the chest, then ran and slide on the floor and grabbed his gun, he pressed a button releasing the old clip and put a new one in, while on his knees then he aimed and fired.

Faith ran around the living room while he fired then ran towards a wall running up it and back flipped off it and turned around just as he fired sending another bullet at her, she pulled out her next hatchet and twirled both of them around with her finger then looked at the man, I counted seven bullets only one left sir, Faith said.

"You're really full of yourself huh, a cocky bitch? I have another clip and you won't beat me, I'm just studying your moves," the man said as he put his gun in a holster on his back and pressed a button on his machete and it split into two. "Hmm nice," Faith said and he charged at her, swung both machetes she used her hatchets to block each attack but each blow was hard and faster and every move she made he was right there.

"Hhhmm he has been studying me, so it was all talk, he knows how I will move." Faith thought to herself as he hit her in the rib twice then upper cut punched her so hard she fell off her feet and on to her back, but she popped back on her feet and continued to fight. She found her opening and flipped backwards and placed her hatchets back in her holster.

"You that cocky you'll put your weapons away?" the man asked.

"No, but this fight is over, I found your disadvantage, your weakness in your fighting style, so it's no point in rushing it. Who sent you? How did you find me? Who are you?" Faith asked and had many more questions, "Like why I keep feeling the chills and where he learn to fight? It it's similar to Black Ice but isn't. He must be a New York nigga," Faith thought to herself as he looked at his black Timberland boots. It was 70 degrees in Houston, Texas no need for boots but a New Yorker will wear Timberlands all year round and he had on a designer belt and jeans and two diamond earring, one in each ear.

Faith scanned the house to see if she could see the little boy again but nothing. He was will hiding in the shadows but she knew he was close by watching, her body felt it. She then looked at the corner of her eye and could see Jainice by the patio door looking for a way into the house. Without warning the man started to attack again, Faith moved side to side dodging his blows. "I told you I don't want to fight, it's over I just want you to answer questions. If you keep going on like this I'll have to kill you." Faith replied.

The man stopped and laughed, his laugher was creepy and dark. "I've killed better fighters and killers than you, and the more I fight you the more I learn." the man said pointing his machete at Faith.

"I believe you but whoever trained you, didn't finish I can tell, you're always in a rush to attack. I was like that and never seen what was in front of me. Now who is the little creepy boy that keeps hiding in the fucking dark? I'm not going to ask you again," Faith said getting pissed off.

"Bitch, fuck you!" the man said and spin kicked Faith so hard it knocked her to the ground, he then jumped on top of her so she couldn't move and began to punch her repeatedly in the face and chest using his legs to pin her arms to the side so she couldn't protect herself. "You talk a lot and all that talking got you nowhere," the man said then stopped punching her when she stared in his eyes.

"I was buying time for you," Faith said and bucked her body and threw him off her.

"But how?" the man said and stood up and started swinging his machetes again trying to slice her in half, to his surprise Faith moved in close on him and punch him in the neck, than his left bicep, making him drop the machete, then his right and he dropped the next machete. Then she kicked him in the dick and punch him in the face. He bent over in pain.

"I give you one thing, it's hard to get you down but not too hard," she said and spin kicked him. He hit the ground sideways groaning in pain. "So, your weakness is that you're big. I was scared to get close to you at first because you know big niggas love that. They get to grab you then it's over, but not you. You're fast and like to punch and kick but wide. So wide my little self just had to move in closer and it's hard for you to hit. Like I told your ass the fight is over." Faith said then kicked him in the stomach. She went to kick him again and he caught her leg.

"The fight is far from over," the man said then the body stepped out the shadow.

Faith turned and looked at him. His skin was smooth as chocolate, he was slim built but the average size for his age, he had a handsome face, but his eyes, his eyes was full of pain as if he had a hard life, but how, he's so young," Faith said to herself but then remember her childhood and looked back down at the man, "Is he beating him like my mother he did me?" Faith then looked back at the boy then seen something else, the boy slowly smiled, his teeth was beautiful and white but his smile was sinister and dark.

"Tazz, go!" he said pointing to Faith then the lager dog came out the shadows and Faith quickly realized it wasn't a dog at all but a hyena. The hyena jumped in the air with his mouth wide open, Faith tried to move but the man had a lock on her leg holding her still. Just before Tazz bit off her face, Egypt jumped up and knocked Tazz out the air and started to attack him. Biting his rib and leg and trying to reach for his neck for a blow, but Tazz fought back as hard as she gave. The two animals rolling in and out the shadows, disappearing and reappearing fighting.

"You know your pet gonna die right," Faith said looking at the boy.

"No he won't." the boy replied with his facial expression twisted up.

"Yea, he will, females are the most ruthless of all creatures, we're the true killers and predators of the animal species."

"She better not kill my Tazz," the boy said then for the first time Faith noticed the holster strapped to his thighs and waist full of chrome knives with black handles. The boy took one out and threw it at Egypt.

"No the fuck you don't, cheating ass," Faith said throwing one of her hatchets knocking the knife out the air. The boy looked at her as if he wanted to chop her head off then pulled out three knives in each hand and throw them at Egypt while she was fighting.

"This little motherfucker," Faith said as she kicked free from the man and pulled out her next

143

hatchet and rolled and pick up the next one, and started hitting the knives out the air. While doing so she could see the boy throw five more at her this time. The more she blocked, the more he kept throwing. Now he was running around in a circle throwing knives at her, Faith blocked them while running after him. "You sore fucking looser and how many of those damn knives you got!" Faith shouted the boy smiled.

"More than you can block." he replied and ran on the wall and threw more knives. Two hit Faith in the stomach she pulled one out and got kick in the back, she hit the floor and dropped her hatchets. She stood up to see both the man and boy standing next to each other looking at her. The man had his machetes and the boy had three throwing knives in each hand. Faith pulled out the second knife and threw it to the ground. "You should've kept that, now you have no weapons," the boy said.

"So what now, y'all going jump me, because neither of you can finish me off by yourselves? This a damn shame and starting to give me a headache and pissing me off and once I'm pissed off I'm gonna kill y'all faster," Faith said.

"You have no weapons but that gun in your holster that got three bullets in it. You gonna find it pretty hard to shoot us, like I said you talk too much. You die tonight." the man said. Faith stretched out her arms and opened her palms and her hatchets flew into her hand. The boy and man looked with their mouths wide opened, "You could do that the whole time but how?" the man said?

Faith took off running and spin kicked the boy in the face knocking him to the ground. I beat kids, you little fucker, then started swinging her hatchets at the man. He couldn't keep up as fast as she was moving trying to bring one of the hatchets on top of his head or face. "Magnets stupid," she said as the guy backpedaled and she threw the hatchet at him and he put his machetes together like an x and blocked it, she opened her palm and the hatchet came back to her. Then she started throwing the hatchets repeatedly at him and catching them while moving closer and closer until the man's back was against the wall, he was forced to stand there just trying to block her blows. "You pissed me the fuck off," Faith said then punched him in the neck, he gasped for air and she went to chop his shoulders off but two of the boys knives hit her hatchet stopping her attack. "You know what?" Faith said punching the man in the face and he dropped to his knees than she turned and chase after the boy.

The boy's eyes open up wide looking at her facial expression full of rage and she running at him at full speed like a football player, it was new to him most people ran from him or was scared of him. But not her, he tried to disappear in the shadows, "No the fuck you don't," Faith said and slid on the wooden floor and kicked his feet from up under him then pop up and start kicking him in the leg and ribs, then sat on the floor and pick him up and threw him over her lap. With the side of her hatchet she swung, hitting him on the ass repeatedly. "I told your ass I beat fucking children and kill them too if they piss me off, if you throw one more fucking knife at me boy I swear I'm gonna jam that knife somewhere the sun don't shine. Am I fucking clear!" Faith said through gritted teeth hitting the boy on the ass again then roll him off her lap, "Remember I beat fucking kids," she said once more kicking him in the stomach. "That's for those two knives that hit me in my stomach bitch." Faith said than ducked just in time as the man tried to slice of her head. Faith rolled her eyes in frustration. "

Why won't they stay the fuck down and stop, if I wanted to really kill them they'd be dead. Faith thought to herself then looked out the corner of her eyes to see Egypt and the hyena still fighting but both was getting tired. Faith tried to spin kick the man then seen the boy pop up with knives in his hand, she looked at him real fast and went back to fighting. He raised his arm to throw the knives but seen Faith eyes and thought of the ass whipping he just got and change his mind and ran up on her and started kicking, "What the fuck," Faith said starting to feel overwhelmed. The boy attacks were fast, the fact that he was short made it hard to hit him, then the man was attacking her at the same. It was just too much, the little boy would leap up in the air and kick her, he bounced around like a frog. Faith tripped over her own leg just as the little boy kicked her and fell on to her back. The boy jammed a knife in each of her hands. Faith tried to move. *"Hmm this is familiar."* Faith thought to herself as she remembered pining Faith to the wall.

"I told you, you underestimate us and talk to me," the man said standing over Faith, then looked at Tazz fighting Egypt, aimed and was about to throw a knife.

"If you hit Egypt with a knife, I'm literally gonna chop your fucking legs off."

The boy stopped and looked at her. "How you're gonna be dead." the boy replied then the man raised his machete high, just as Jainice and two henchmen bust through the patio door and six more henchmen came through windows upstairs of the house and now stood on the staircase pointing guns at the man and little boy.

Faith looked up at him. "Looks like you're coming with me, I was just killing time." Faith said then looked at Jainice use darts, "I want them alive," Faith said then pulled her hands through the knife, the little boy and the man watched in amazement as she stood up and her hands healed. Then she looked at them front and back.

"You was faking it, acting like we had you? You're just like him and you been holding back," the man said.

"Well yea, I kind been holding back, but I can say the same for the two of you, but yes I been faking giving my men enough time to take you down but we will have enough time to talk later." Faith said and turned her back then walked off to join Cricket and Jainice, the man looked at the little boy. The little boy grinned an evil smile and start throwing knives, two of them hit a hen in the forehead going through his mask, another one hit a henchmen in his chest as the man pulled out what looked like a grenade and pulled the pin and drop it in front of him, black smoke came out, making everyone cough and making it impossible for anyone to see, Faith turn around. "What the fuck now?" she said as one of her henchmen's body was thrown at her and landed by her feet. "You need light, use the light on your guns!" Faith shouted.

"What's happening?" Jainice asked.

"They move funny in the dark, I don't know how yet but it's not normal and you can't see them, their using the smoke to blind us from their attack," Faith said as a knife hit the neck of one of the henchmen standing next to her.

"This some bullshit, we need to kill them, they're too dangerous to try and catch." Cricket said.

"No, I want them alive." Faith replied and heard another one of her henchmen scream as his arm went flying in the air, the man with machete swung again and chopped off the henchmen head.

"Uhmm bitch, I don't know who they are but they're going through your henchmen like a box of chicken from Popeyes, eating everything up. I don't think you're gonna be able to take them alive," Jainice said.

Faith knew it was true. "Shoot them," Faith said and the henchmen put the dart guns away and grabbed their Mp5 machine guns that was strapped to their shoulders, and sent a hail of bullets into the smoke.

"We got to go," the man said and threw another smoke grenade as bullets flew pass his head, he reloaded his gun and fired the .50 caliber bullet hit a henchmen in the head and exploded.

"Oh shit, what the fuck is he shooting?" Cricket said looking at the henchmen on the top of the stairs case with no head and his body falling.

The man scooped up the boy in his arms and threw him toward the patio door, the boy looked like a missile heading toward Faith and the four henchmen behind her, he threw knives killing two instantly then hit the floor rolling and stabbed Faith in the leg and Jainice in the stomach, "I didn't throw it, mean bitch," he said then ran and jump on a henchmen's arm and stabbed him in the side of his head, as his body fell the boy screamed "Tazz." The hyena stopped fighting Egypt and ran toward the boy, the boy jumped on to his back as if he was a horse and said "Run," riding him out the patio back door.

Jainice and Faith looked. "Well, you don't see that every fucking day," Jainice said as she pulled out the knife in her stomach.

Faith turned around to see she was face to face with the chrome Desert Eagle handgun. The henchmen was spread out in the house shooting blindly, and coughing. Cricket was in the dining room and ran over and side kicked the man, and swung to punch him but the man blocked his blow and grab him by the neck and pick him up by it as if he was nothing. Faith pulled out her gun as her heart raced. "Up until now, I wanted you and the boy alive, but if you hurt him I will kill you and the brat I promise you." Faith said meaning every word. As she aimed for the man's head, he slowly moved his back toward the patio door, keeping Faith and Jainice in front of him.

"I told you we should've killed him," Jainice said as she pulled out her gun.

"If you continue his work, we will be back and now I know what to expect and how to handle you, if we can handle him, we sure as hell handle you, you move like him but your no Black Ice. He would've tried to kill me right away, you hesitated." The man said.

"You did too, it don't have to be any issues between us, now let my friend go or I'll make sure my pets eat that boy." Faith said.

"What happens to any one that follows you is on you," the man said.

"Listen, put him down. I don't give a fuck about nothing you're saying right now, but may you put friend down. Faith said through clench teeth and rage in her eyes.

"He shouldn't have tried to save you the man said and lifted Cricket higher and squeeze the trigger, sending a bullet into Cricket's chest and another in his stomach, then dropped him while running and firing behind him.

"Nooooooo!" Faith screamed as his body dropped to the ground. Faith ran after the man shooting until her gun emptied and then she grabbed a Mp5 machine gun off a dead henchmen's body and ran outside, chasing the man through the backyard. She aimed and sent a hail of bullets toward his back, he rolled forward and got back up, than hopped a fence into another yard, Faith followed close behind, climbing over the fence. He then used his body weight to break down the back door to someone's house and ran inside and Faith ran in after him. He continued to run straight and broke down the front door and was outside once again. "I'm gonna fucking kill you, I swear." Faith screamed as imagine of the man shooting Cricket played in her mind. She fought back her tears, aimed, and squeeze the trigger, sending a bullet into the back of the man's leg, he stumble forward and ran up to a black min van and hopped in. "No! No you don't get away!" Faith screamed while sending bullets in the mini-van as it sped down the block, the back window broke open, and Faith could see the little boy and Tazz just staring at her. The little boy stuck up his middle finger and stuck out his tongue as the van turned around the corner.

"Fuck!" Faith said and ran back around the block to the abandon house to see her henchmen already cleaning up, getting rid of bullet shells and lighting fireworks. "Where's Cricket?" Faith asked.

"He was still alive but barely, we need to get out of here, the men gonna blow the house up and make it seem like it was fireworks that everyone was hearing, and we gonna dart a few neighbors And let them sleep fir a few days , this will blow over but we can't stay in this town no more," Jainice said as they walked around the block back to their houses. Faith held her head down. "You was playing with them I was watching, you could've stopped them a few times Faith and you didn't even use half your strength," Jainice said.

"My father said to never use what the formula gave me like that, never show it off, I was holding back for that reason and the other reason was I was trying to see what was the point of them attacking me, and I underestimated them because I thought I could take them alive." Faith replied.

"That's not a good answer. Cricket could die. I don't think he's gonna make it, the caliber of the bullet that guy was shooting are too big. Who was those guys and why did they have a hyena?" Jainice asked mad that they shot Cricket and even madder that Faith didn't just shoot them right away instead of playing with them, not understanding her motive. Jainice pulled out a blunt and lit it and took three pulls, then passed it to Faith.

Faith inhaled a few times and held the smoke in and exhaled letting it out slowly while crying. "I hope Cricket don't die and I think we just met some of my father's children, I think they're my brothers and they won't stop coming for me until I kill them or they kill me." Faith said then looked up to the sky.

Chapter 6

The smell of urine was strong, it made Meashell's nose itch. She opened her eyes to see she was in a dark room inside a cage, she tried to stand up but couldn't the cage was too small. "I was wondering when you'd get up." She heard a voice say and realized it came from a cage next to her, she crawled over and was shocked to see who it was,

"How are you still alive?" Meashell asked.

"I think I pissed the pretty dark-skin lady off when I tried to stab her in the back. The crazy thing is they been feeding me and even fixed my leg, I should've done bled to death." the man said.

Meashell looked at him, "This can't be, I left you for dead Fabio, and if she kept you alive that's not a good sign, she's gonna feed us to those damn hyenas." Meashell replied.

"Maybe, maybe not. I made peace with my life and what's to come in that cave, so it is what it is. No reason to cry or get depressed about it or angry." Fabio replied.

"It sounds like you gave up, I'm not giving up, fuck that," Meashell said.

"Maybe that's why they keep shooting you with those darts every time you wake up. They know you're gonna fight or try to escape," Fabio said.

"Keep shooting me?" Meashell said to herself then remembered every time she opened her eyes she felt sleepy, she looked down at the pants she had on, they was soaked. The smell of urine she had smelled earlier was coming from herself. She looked back over at Fabio. "How long have I been a sleep?" she asked.

"It's hard to tell, there's no light in this room to tell when night and day is and they took my watch and phone but they feed me twice a day, so if I was to count by the meals, now this is me just guessing because I don't know how long I been asleep but I'll say seven days," Fabio said as the room door opened and a henchmen came in with two trays of food and bottles of water. "Oh shit, we get curry goat tonight and lobster tail. I love it here," Fabio said as the henchmen slid the tray of food in his cage then slid Meashell's food to her.

"Wait! I want to talk to Faith or Jainice," Meashell said. The henchmen turned around.

"They will speak to you when their ready, now eat!" The henchmen said and walked out the room. Meashell looked at Fabio, he wasted no time to dig in, sucking of the curry goat bones after eating the meat off them and then opening the water and drinking it.

"You're not scared they're gonna to poison you? Meashell asked. Not believing the way he was eating like he had no cares in the world and was in a five star hotel.

"Like I told you, I made peace with myself and everything else, I doubt they will poison me. I made the pretty black woman too mad for that, beside you use to be one of them, is poison something they used?" Fabio said while sucking on another curry goat bone then eating some rice.

"No poison is not how they will kill us, it's not painful enough. But it's hard for me to eat, I'm worried and scared, got a thousand things on my mind, like what they going do to me, can I escape, where the hell I'm at, the last location was destroyed, so what compound is this, will Minglee come for me? I thought about all of that." Meashell said.

"Hmm, I see why they kept you asleep," Fabio said picking up his lobster tail and taking a bite out of it, Kool-Aid would be perfect right now, but they always give me water, pssst," Fabio said while sucking his teeth.

Meashell bust out laughing and her stomach started to growl, she stuffed a couple of spoons of rice in her mouth, then ate some curry goat. "Want to hear some crazy shit?" Meashell asked.

"Sure." Fabio replied.

"These people promote healthy fucking eating, that's why they give you water. I was with them for two years and we get soda every four mouths. They don't play about that shit," Meashell said.

"So why you leave and what you did do to piss uhmm... what's her name off so bad that she kidnapped and kill a whole village?" Fabio said while drinking water. "I should've told the guard I need hot sauce but he's not gonna come back now, this one meaner than the one from the other day," Fabio said.

Meashell look at him as if he was crazy. Fabio wasn't as big as everyone else in his village and was an older man, in his forties, with black hair that he kept cut short. His brown-skin seemed to glow. *"How can this man be this calm and relaxed."* Meashell thought to herself. "I pissed the bitch off, her name is Faith, because I spit on her and when she was dying I kinda beat her some more and left her for dead. I actually watched the building crush her and my ex-best friend to death. Thought I finally escaped this place after two years, I really thought it would be her father coming after me, he's worse. He don't have a conscious or empathy for people. Faith's weakness is she feels sorry for everyone or bad she did a certain thing." Meashell replied and started sucking on some curry goat bone.

"Well damn, I tried to stab her in the back because she told me to die peacefully or get eaten; you spit on her and left her for dead, oh yea she really gonna want to hurt you, why she waiting?" Fabio said after finishing all the food on his plate.

"I don't know but do they put the people they take asleep while traveling," Meashell said.

"So what gonna happen to our people in the village?" Fabio asked and for the first time looked sad.

"She's gonna sale them overseas, if she haven't already, they barely keep people. Sometimes they keep the women, but not always, it's less headaches for them to just sale them all at once," Meashell said.

"What about the kids, she also took a lot of our children?" Fabio asked.

"I don't know, she never took children before, her father don't as well. Shit, in fact when the women that do stay here get pregnant he let them go if they feel they're not gonna talk, most won't. I don't know what Faith will do with the children, but know we need to worry about ourselves and escape," Meashell said.

"Ain't worrying about yourself is what got you into this mess and dragged the rest of us with you?" Fabio said.

"I liked it better when I was asleep, I didn't have to listen to you," Meashell said studying the cage for a loose screw or anything she use as a weapons.

"I liked it better when you was asleep too." Fabio replied.

The medical center was designed just like a hospital. Faith had three doctors and two nurses treating the injured men. She walked to Cricket's room, he was on life support, with a ventilator breathing for him. The .50 caliber bullet had broken his lower spine and also destroyed one of his lungs making the other one collapse. He sat in the bed with his eyes open barely able to move. Faith grabbed his hand, Cricket was brown-skin complexion and not the best looker, in his warily thirty but he was loyal ever since the day she spared his life. Faith grabbed his hand as the doctor walked in, he was a bald head older Indian doctor with glasses and white shirt but with a nice smile, "What's the update?" Faith asked.

"I'm sorry to tell you this Mistress, but his heart rate is dropping and so is his blood pressure, he's not gonna make it, we tried everything. The fight is up to him now, those bullets did severe damage, to be honest, I've never met anyone live this long from being shot with a .50 caliber close range gun. From what I'm told he saved your life. If that man was to have shot you in the head with that gun, there'd be nothing left of your head, so your healing wouldn't work. Cricket knew that when he attacked that man." Doctor Rashi said.

"How you know all of that, how you know that's exactly what happened?" Faith replied.

"Because I'm smart and the other henchmen talk, telling me how they got injured when I treat them. It was quite a few that had knives stuck in them and no one that got shot with that man's gun survived," Doctor Rashi said.

Faith pulled out her Glock 26 and aimed it at Doctor Rashi without looking. "You save him or I'll kill you, use my blood, it will heal him," Faith said.

"Mistress it don't work like that, whatever's in your blood bonded with your DNA and cells, I'm a doctor not a geneticist which you have by the way, to break down the virus in your system that helps you heal but I'm afraid to tell you, you don't have much time he'll be dead in a day or two," Doctor Rashi said.

Faith put away her gun. She looked into Cricket eyes, it was as if he was trying to tell her something, she looked down at his hand that had an i.v needle in it and it was moving as if he was trying to write. Faith knew the big tube stuffed down his throat to keep him breathing was preventing him from speaking. She pulled out her cellphone and opened up and note app. "Here text it, whatever you got to say." Faith said putting the phone in his weak hand. Doctor Rashi stood on the other side of the room by the door just watching as Cricket used all his strength to bring the phone to his face and started texting. A few seconds later he passed the phone back to Faith.

Faith looked at the note and start reading, "I failed you once and I'm sorry as bad I couldn't fail you again, I said I'll never leave your side but I can't keep that promise Mistress. I'm in pain, it hurts, and what kind of life would I have if my legs and lower half don't work, if my dick don't work lol, that's not a life for me, even if you was able to give me the formula in time I'll still be a cripple, no thank you, I'm ready to go, I'm not scared. It's been an honor being by your side, thank you for sparing my life that day. Now please pull the fucking plug now. Love Cricket." Faith eyes fill with tears and looked up at Cricket crying.

"No I'm not going to do it, I can save you, I can save you somehow, so what if your dick don't work, you'll still be here. I need you. Who I'm gonna find that's loyal like you, this the second time you ran into bullets for me, without hesitation. I need you here Cricket. Cricket shook his head no and snatched the phone and started to text and passed it back.

Faith read, "Pull the pull plug, kill me! Kill me please don't leave me like this please my friend kill me." Faith read the text and cried uncontrollably then looked at Cricket crying. She bent over and kissed him on the forehead, then went over to the ventilator machine and bent down and pulled out the plug. The machine shut off and stopped breathing for Cricket, his chest no longer went up and down.

He looked at Faith one last time and somehow managed to say "Thank you!" with the tube in his throat as he died. Faith lay on his chest crying hysterically. The more she wiped her tears with the back of her hand the more would come.

Then she heard doctor Rashi voice say, "You did the right thing." Faith looked up and her eyes was red as she walked over to Doctor Rashi. "Wait! I'm the best doc you got here, don't do nothing hasty. I just said you did the right thing." Faith chopped him in the neck with the side of her hand, and pulled out her Glock 26 and aimed down and squeezed. The bullet shattered Doctor Rashi's kneecap into pieces. He dropped to his right knee while holding his left screaming. Two henchmen rushed into the room and Faith looked up at them, "Take him to the zoo and stop his bleeding first," Faith said and walked off. She stormed out the medical center and down the hallway to Lefty's private room and bust in to see him on a couch crying. Faith stopped in her track , and didn't know what to do.

Lefty looked up, "I see you must've pulled the plug, he ask me to do it this morning and I couldn't, I couldn't no matter how he said he was in pain, he was my best friend like a brother to me. You probably in here wondering why I wasn't there, but I couldn't watch him go Faith, I couldn't." Lefty said while crying.

Faith could tell he'd been crying all day, his black velvet couch had tear stains on it and Lefty didn't look like himself. He wasn't much to look at, he was short, fat and dark-skin but kept himself clean and well-taken care of, his hair wasn't cut, his bread out-grown, needed cut and he just looked a mess in sweat pants and a Nike shirt. *"Damn he's right, I came in here to take my anger out on him, never considering what he lost or going through I was just mad he wasn't there for Cricket's last moment, but now I understand why he wouldn't want to see it, look what it's done to me. I just want to lash out, hurt something or anyone."* Faith thought to herself. Faith walked over to Lefty and kissed him on the forehead. "I want you to find all my father's children that's older than me and around my age," Faith said.

"All of them, you do now that man have babies like a rabbit right, I don't think even he keeps track of all of them Look how long it took him to find you." Lefty replied.

"Find them all and find the two that did this to our friend our brother, we gonna take something from them, like they took something from us. I want them to feel what we feel right now." Faith said and walked away.

Lefty wiped his tears, "Yes, they will feel pain for what they did to Cricket."

Faith turned around and said, "Upgrade the men's armor, find something that damn .50 caliber bullet can't go through."

"That's gonna be just as hard as finding all Black Ice kids." Lefty mumbled.

Fabio lay on his back with his knee in the air rocking it side by side and his hand behind his head. The room door opened and Meashell sat up. "Tell Faith I need to talk! Tell Jainice! One of them need to speak to me!" Meashell shouted as two henchmen walked to Fabio's cage.

"Come on," a henchmen said opening the cage and grabbing Fabio by the arm. "I guess I'll see you later," Fabio said as he walked with the henchmen.

"Did you hear me, tell them I need to talk." Meashell shouted.

One of the henchmen turned around and looked at Meashell, "Your time is coming traitor, just hope I get to be the one on guard duty and get to feed you, and spit on you. I signed up for it, I pray the Mistress picks me and we get to spend more time together." The henchmen said and turned back around.

"Fuck you!" Meashell shouted.

"So they're going keep me alive a little longer in this cage; perfect gives me enough time to think of a way to escape this place. All they got to do is let me out this cage once or twice, and I can kill the henchmen, the only one that can stop me is Faith, Jainice, Lefty and Cricket, but it seems like they got their hands full," Meashell said to herself and laid back down.

Fabio was led to an all-white room, he could see an Indian naked man a little older than him strapped into a steel chair panicking. Fabio was strapped to the chair next to him. Fabio turned his head and looked at the Indian man, he had on a white lab coat, with a name tag that said Doctor Rashi. "So doc what are you in here for? Me I stab the Queen in the back well I tried to," Fabio said.

Doctor Rashi turned his head and looked at Fabio as if he'd lost his mind. "Are you crazy sir?" Doctor Rashi asked.

"No, but some people say I have a dry sense of humor." Fabio replied.

"Well sir, there's nothing funny about this situation at all, I rather die than what she's gonna do to us," doctor Rashi said with fear in his voice.

"Hmm, it must be bad if it got the doc scared, but hey I lived a good life, a full life of joy and the last meal they gave me was great." Fabio said.

"I wish I could look at things like you sir but we about to enter hell and the devil isn't a man but a woman named Faith." Doctor Rashi replied.

"Damn that was deep, look at it this way, they kill us then it's over with, they keep us alive that means more good food. The way they feed their people in this place is amazing, I hope to meet the chef one day." Fabio responded.

"You're missing a few brain cells, I'm sure of it. You have no idea what this place is or who we dealing with, talking to you making my stomach hurt. Please don't speak to me no more sir, thank you," Doctor Rashi said and turned his head back straight.

"Okay, rude ass," Fabio said as the room door opened and Faith came in followed by two henchmen and a nurse. Fabio looked and could see one henchmen holding a double blade axe and another a blow torch, then a nurse wearing a pink uniform. The henchmen brought Faith the double blade axe.

"I'm sorry Mistress, please don't do this, I'm one of the best doctors you have, I didn't mean nothing by what I said. I'm sorry, please just let me go back to work. I learned my lesson," Doctor Rashi said as Faith walked toward him without saying a word.

Faith looked at him and was stuck in a trance, day dreaming. She was there but not there all she seen was her brother holding Cricket up by the neck with one hand and the barrel of his gun pressed against Cricket's chest. In slow motion she could she chunks of flesh fly out the back of Cricket as the bullet exited his body. "Nooooooo!" Faith screamed like a mad woman, then swung chopping off Doctor Rashi's right leg, then swung again chopping off his right leg.

"Ahhhh!" Doctor Rashi screamed in agonizing pain. Faith was getting ready to swing again.

"Mistress, you're moving too fast, if you chop off the rest of his limbs before you stop the bleeding, he will die." the nurse said.

Faith snapped back into reality and looked at Doctor Rashi screaming and crying and blood pouring out his legs. She looked at the henchmen with the blow torch. He heated up her axe and she pressed it against Doctor Rashi's right leg.

"Oh shit! Oh shit!" Fabio screamed while watching. "Fuck no!" he said and started squirming around in the chair, "This is not cool, that's not a good way to go, hell no! Shoot me! Stab me, piss on me but don't chop me the fuck up!" Fabio shouted.

"Shhh, quiet your turn coming soon." Faith said looking at him as she pressed the hit axe on Doctor Rashi's right leg. She looked at the nurse then all the blood on the white floor it was going down the drain. "He's a heavy bleeder, order two more blood bags for the transfusion I don't want him to die, I got carried away.

"Yes Mistress," the nurse said and left the room. Doctor Rashi finally stopped crying and screaming. "Please no more I'm sorry, I should've kept my mouth shut." Doctor Rashi replied.

"It wasn't the fact you should've kept your mouth shut, you was right Doctor I did the right thing. You're here for two reasons; one, I'm credibly pissed off at the world and you happened to be the object of my distraction and pain, and two, if I was my father you wouldn't have even spoken to me, just did your job. So, I'm wondering is everyone here thinking I'm soft, cause I run things a little differently? Do I got to kill a few of y'all so you can get the picture that I'm nothing to fuck with. My father did say it's better to rule with fear than love. Now look at me, one of the people I loved that takes a bullet for me twice is dead. What if I never love him like a brother, would I be able to kill my real brother faster when he grabbed Cricket?" Faith said out loud talking to herself.

"It sounds like you need therapy, no matter what you did the outcome will be the same, the only difference is you built a friendship that helped built your character more not weaken it, you learned from this Cricket and he became a brother, don't you give those memories up," Fabio said.

Faith turned around and looked at him as if he'd lost his mind. "Yea, yea, no matter what I'm gonna get chopped up so I might as well speak freely, shit the worse is already gonna happen to me. So like I asked would you give those memories up or better yet any memories from the friends you made just because they was killed, murdered, or just die? Fabio asked.

Faith stood quiet for a second thinking about all the time she spent with Cricket, training with him and laughing, then thinking about Jainice the time they spend together always talking smoking and Lefty always listening to her and helping her run things. "Would I give those memories and times up to be harder and colder? Faith said to herself then looked at Fabio. "No I wouldn't, I cherish them," Faith said.

"I know you do, I just wanted to point that out real fast before you go back to chopping up old doc over there and kill me." Fabio replied.

Faith looked at him. "You're a weird man, I actually like you but could never trust you. You literally tried to stab me in the back, but I tell you what, I'm gonna let you keep your tongue and hearing so we can talk more. I think I'll use you as my therapist," Faith said as the nurse returned with another henchmen who held four blood bags and some tools for the nurse.

"Keep my tongue?" Fabio said confuse.

"You'll see." Faith replied and swung her axe chopping off the doctor left arms right above the elbow.

"Ahhhh! I thought he calmed you down and made valid points about losing friends that the memories are still there!" Doctor Rashi screamed in pain.

"He did, but I'm still angry just a little and we already started. My father said, "Don't start something and don't finish it," "Now we can't have anyone thinking my father didn't raise me right. So I got to finish what I started." Faith said as the torch heated up the axe and she pressed it on to the doctor's skin, binding the wounds closed. Doctor Rashi passed out from the pain and the nurse ran over and checked his pulse.

"His heart rate good and so is his blood pressure." the nurse said as she pulled out the long syringe with adrenaline in it and prepared to jam it in the doctors' heart.

"No don't, let him sleep. I kinda feel bad for him." Faith said and the nurse moved and Faith swung again, chopping off his right arm, Then binding it closed. The doctor didn't flinch or move an inch. He was knocked out cold. Faith dropped the axe and sat on his lap. Fabio continued to watch Faith open the doctor's mouth and pulled out his tongue as far as it could go and turned her head and smile at Fabio as she pulled out her knife and slowly sawed the tongue off and threw it on the floor.

Fabio's body jerked as he vomited, throwing up on himself and the floor. "What the fuck wrong with you? he asked?

"Watch yourself, I told you I'll let you keep your tongue don't over-do it with your mouth or let it get you in more trouble than you can handle." Faith said as she grabbed the long chrome needle that looked like an ice pick and pushed it into the doctor right ear until his ear drum popped and blood and wax dripped out his ear. She then did it to his left ear. After Faith was finished she hopped off his lap and the nurse and henchmen quickly went to work. The nurse sewed up his tongue while the henchmen collected the chopped of body parts off the floor and mopped up some of the blood. The nurse then hooked the doctor up to an i.v, one for blood and the next for antibiotics and fluids.

Fabio couldn't believe his eyes. "This some mad science bullshit. I don't care what you say, this isn't normal," Fabio said.

Faith picked back up the axe and let it drag on the floor as she walked toward Fabio until she was standing in front of him. "You got to ask yourself what's normal these days, nothing really is. So Fabio, are you a screamer or a crier?" Faith asked.

"Huh?" Fabio replied looking nervous.

"I ask are you a screamer or a crier? You know what let's just find out," Faith said and swung chopping off his right arm.

"Ahhhh! Ahhhh!" Fabio screamed at the top of his lungs and struggled to break free from the chair but his left arm was strapped down in the arm rest and his legs was strapped to the steel chair legs, he rocked back and forth hoping he could break the chair somehow but it was bolted to the ground. "Ahhhh!" he continued to scream.

"You're definitely a screamer my friend," Faith said as she looked at the axe turn hot red from the blow torch then placed it on to Fabio's arm burning the wound closed.

"Please! Please!" Fabio screamed and sounded like he was singing in a church choir. "Please stop, no more! Just kill me please no more!" he screamed.

"It's almost over, we got three more to go," Faith said then swung again chopping off his next arm while smiling as if she was playing baseball.

"You're sick! This is sick! What's wrong with you? What wrong with you people letting her do this?" Fabio said looking at the nurse and four henchmen in the room.

Faith pressed the hot axe to his left arm until she smelled burnt hotdog and removed it. "Well, my father's a fucking serial killer, but that's no excuse? It's something in me that tells me to do things, like an evil little voice. It says kill that person, chop up that person." Faith replied.

"And you fucking listen to it?" Fabio said with drool flying out his mouth.

"Yea, most times it be right." Faith responded.

"We all have a voice, don't mean we listen to it. You have no impulse control, you just do what the voice say? So who's in charge? Fabio shouted.

"Well the voice of course," Faith said swinging again chopping off his left leg, "Here batter, batter, what's the saying with baseball? It's a home run! Right?" Faith asked as the axe heated up then she placed it on his leg but Fabio held his scream in and just stared at her with hate and a running nose.

"I knew I liked you, most people don't make it to three without passing out, shit my bitch ass baby daddy got one limb chopped and passed the fuck out. Surprisingly, my mother is the only one I've seen take it like a gangster like you doing so far," Faith said.

"Just fucking kill me and get it over with the pain is too much to bare," Fabio said.

"Nah, kill you, never. I enjoy your company. You say what you want and don't give a fuck, most people are too scared of me to speak their mind, except my close friends Jainice, Lefty and Cricket and J-Money. Now I only got two left?" Faith said getting sad thinking of J-Money and Cricket's death. Then swung twice chopping off both Fabio legs, then dropped the axe. Burn his legs closed and give him and the doctor some morphine for the pain and put gag balls in their mouths then bring me Meashell when you're done." Faith ordered and went to the corner of the room and sat on the floor Indian style and watched the henchmen work, collecting Fabio's body parts and burning his legs, she dazed out and couldn't even hear him screaming "No more!" as she touched her stomach thinking of her baby. *"Everything going wrong, my baby gone and I'm down to two people I trust and love, it's like I keep losing people and don't know what to do. I can't hide because problems will find me, how can I keep Lefty, Jainice, Egypt and Raven safe? I'm gonna have to do something, my father made running things look so easy, he did it like it was nothing."* Faith thought to herself while holding her stomach, hugging herself. The smell of burnt flesh lingered in the air.

Faith lifted her head and felt Jainice hand on her shoulder, Jainice sat down next to her, "I know you're stressing over Cricket's death, we all are. Everyone took it hard, even a lot of the henchmen but we gonna get passed this. Here eat this," Jainice said passing Faith some gummy worms.

"I'm not in the mood for junk." Faith replied.

"Girl shut the hell up and eat this," Jainice said Faith looked at her and smile because she was one of the only people in the world that spoke to her like that and knew better and just didn't give a fuck. Faith took four gummy worms out the pack and threw them in her mouth, then grabbed two more. "Slow down these sweets strong as hell, like 250 mg for each gummy. Jainice replied.

"Strong as hell, what are they?" Faith asked.

"Weed gummy edibles, but you'll see when that shit hit, it's gonna hit hard." Jainice replied and smiled.

"You always trying to get me fucked up. I don't know why I trust eating anything from you," Faith said.

"Because you know whatever I give you, gonna have you laughing your ass off." Jainice said.

"I don't feel nothing, maybe they don't work on me, but I was thinking of ways to keep Lefty safe I'm gonna have the geneticist analyze your blood, see if we can separate your cells from the formula and give it to him, Egypt and Raven then I won't lose no more friends," Faith said. That sounds like a good idea but we still have to watch out for shotguns and people like your brother with machetes and swords or that damn hand cannon your brother called a damn gun, that shit blows a henchmen head straight the fuck off, solute it into tiny pieces." Jainice said as the gummy started to kick in.

"Yea but anything to increase your survival rate is good. I'm starting to feel funny, like my whole body feeling warm," Faith said as she laid on the floor and start giggling.

"Told you, this a different kinda of high. You gonna feel it in your whole body and mind this time," Jainice said laying on the floor next to her and started laughing as she floated in and out of reality.

Meashell continued to twist the screw on the side of the cage. She had been working at it for a day now. "Yes, I got it," she said as the steel screw came out, just as a henchmen entered the room.

"It's your turn, I can't wait, I swear when she's done with you and no one's around and I'm on guard duty you're all mine beloved." the henchmen said.

"Yea, we'll see." Meashell replied as soon as he opened the cage, *"I'm gonna break his neck,"* Meashell thought to herself then seen him raise his hand and had a dart gun. "No wait!" Meashell shouted.

"You think anyone's stupid enough to transport you anywhere without you being knock out." the henchmen laugh then shot her with a dart.

"No," Meashell said and lost consciousness. The sound of laughter in the room was loud even in her sleep, Meashell opened her eyes, "My fucking head is throbbing," she said to herself then quickly looked around to study her environment. She could see Faith and Jainice laughing and giggling on the floor next to the door, the room was all white even the floor. She turned her head to see two more chains. With white sheets covering then up that was sitting in them. She noticed the i.v bags on stands next to each chair, one bag looked like blood and the other Meashell couldn't make out.

Meashell tried to turn her head all the way around as it can go to see what was behind her, it looked like tall cages with a black curtains on them but she couldn't make it out. Meashell than felt the screw, it was still in her hand, she held on to it even when she was asleep, she looked down at the straps that held her to the chair to see that they was leather. She started rubbing the screw against the strap on her right wrist, *"Okay, I just need to buy time, it will take me a few seconds but I can break free and whatever those two are on is gonna help me a lot. They're high as hell right now."* Meashell thought to herself while rubbing the screw faster and harder against her strap.

"Man, we got to stop playing," Faith said while smiling.

"Why bitch, you know you floating just like I am." Jainice replied.

"Yea, but look," Faith said pointing to Meashell.

"Oh shit, I almost forgot they brought that bitch in here. Hmmm, you should let me do it! I want to try it," Jainice said while smiling from ear to ear.

"How about we both do it and I have another great idea," Faith said.

"What?" Jainice replied.

"You'll see," Faith said while trying to stand up on her feet."

"Yo, I'm never eating them gummies again, my body feel so damn funny. I'm hot as hell, my heart racing, it's like every part of me is high unlike when I smoke, it's more in my head. Yea, I get tired or hungry but nothing like this. I'm fucking horny, my pussy mad wet yo, and I got a lot of energy out of nowhere," Faith said.

"You'll get use to it, now let's go play with Meashell grimy ass," Jainice said while trying to stand up.

"What the fuck they talking about, doing what to me?" Meashell thought to herself and continued to rub the screw on the leather strap, she looked down at it and seen that it started to cut through, making a little rip. She hurried up and hoped Faith and

Jainice hadn't seen what she was doing but they was in a world of their own.

Faith stumbled to the door and held the wall, "It feels like everything fucking spinning," she said. Then called a henchmen, "Bring the nurse and three men and the girls," Faith ordered.

"The girls? What's she talking about? But if she brings the nurse that would explain the i.v hooked up to whoever up under those sheets." Meashell thought to herself as Faith and Jainice walked over to her.

"To think I use to love you, you was like a sister to me," Jainice said.

"Yea I bet, and look how fast you replaced me with miss crazy right there." Meashell replied.

"I never replaced you, we was all family until you left me to die and jumped me, you literally tried to beat my ass, the only reason you stopped was because the building was coming down, that type of hate just don't come out of nowhere, it's something you was holding on to and been wanted to do and the opportunity just presented itself. The love I had for you wasn't the same as the love you had for me, so stop the bullshit." Jainice said.

"You're always a philosopher and therapist when you're high but maybe you're right, I always wanted to beat your ass," Meashell said.

"But why? I don't understand, I was always there for you." Jainice asked confused.

"Because you was always there, you always had the nicest apartments, the newest truck that just came out, dress nicer, had to be that bitch every time one of us fell off, it was you there helping us, love life, you was every place everything, it was as if you made me feel little or as if I wasn't doing something right," Meashell said.

"I don't understand, I never tried to make you feel little you was my friend, I was supposed to help you and the others when needed, shit I'll like that help if something happened to me." Jainice replied.

"That's the point you never tried to belittle anyone, you just came off perfect. Shit, I wish you did fall off, just so I can say I helped you for once in life. So I can have one over your head," Meashell said while slowly rubbing the screw against the leather, knowing they wasn't looking at her hands.

"Damn it sound like she was hating on you for being a good person, now you see why I'm not a good person," Faith said than laughed "But for real, this what it means to have girl friends or friend that secretly despise you for who you are or your lifestyle, cause to me it sounds as if she's mad that you didn't have the same issues as her and the other girls, mad you had nice things and what's even more stupid is she is mad because you was there for her. That part I don't get, but you can be there for me friend, I won't be mad." Faith said while laughing and touching Jainice shoulder.

"Ugh, it's more than that, I can't put it to words, but Jainice made you want to be her and she always saved money, always had men that gave her anything she wanted without asking, so deep down I wanted to be her and hated her for it. So, yes that day I got to beat her and knew she was dying I was glad, all the years of watching her grow better and better to finally see her on her fucking knees, weak, crying and I was the strong one, the smart one, that shit felt good." Meashell replied.

"Damn bitches really be acting like they're your friends but really your enemy. I don't want no new girlfriend. I just learned a lot today, shit blowing my high." Faith said.

"Yea, people do that but I never thought Dallas, Meashell, Tammy or Minglee felt that way, I thought they was my sisters." Jainice said lowering her head.

"Bitch, don't let this two dollar hoe get you upset, shit be happy she showed her true colors, instead waiting for the last second when you really need her and then you would've been fucked. Here eat two of these gummy's," Faith said and passed Jainice the pack of gummy worms. Jainice stuffed two in her mouth and Faith did the same. Faith moved closer to Meashell and looked her in the eyes, "The crazy part is my father seen the snake in your ass and I didn't, he said "Those aren't no good daughter, don't trust them, trust Cricket, Left , Jainice and J-Money, the rest kill or feed to the hyenas." I guess today I'm finally gonna listen to my pops." Faith said smiling hard as the gummies started to kick back in and two henchmen entered the room with two little girls wearing blue dresses.

Meashell couldn't make out who they was. I really wanted to start and go first, she hurt my feelings I'm not gonna lie," Jainice said.

"I understand, but I want to see if they'll pass the test. Once there done, then you can have fun, I don't blame you for wanting to hurt her, the things she said hurt more than that bitch kicking me and spitting on me," Faith said and waved the girls over.

Meashell eyes opened wider, then she looked at Faith. "Hey girls, say hi to your auntie," Faith said while smiling. Kaia and Lani just looked at Meashell with tears in their eyes.

"Girls you're okay, thank God Meashell said.

"No thanks to you, you left my sister then left me for the hyenas to get us all so you could get away," Kaia said.

"No, no baby that's not what happened, I was leaving you then I was gonna come back for you both." Meashell responded.

"No, you lie," Kaia said.

Faith smiled and looked at Meashell, "You're a grimy bitch, just left those girls to die but it's okay now, I'll raise them their mine and so are all the other children from the village but these two will be trained by me and kept close to me, so I thank you," Faith said.

"So you gonna train them to be killers, a monster like you bitch?" Meashell shouted.

"Yep and why do you care acting all mad you left them, was hoping by us killing them you'd have more time to escape, shit you even shot a guy in the leg to get away. But we will get into that in a minute. Since you killed J-Money I wanted to do

186

something different to you than the others, make you pay more and suffer," Faith said.

"Get on with it already! I don't care what you do bitch. I'll never scream, I won't cry, or beg so do your worse!" Meashell shouted. Faith pulled out her hatchet from her holster on the back of her belt and passed it to one of the henchmen, he heated the blade with the blow torch then passed it back to Faith. "Go head bitch!" Meashell said.

"Oh it's not my turn yet," Faith said and turned around to Kaia and Lina, "Girls, just like we practiced on that guy, it's time." Faith said and handed Kaia the handle, then Lani grabbed the handle as well, they both moved slowly toward Meashell.

"Wait! What? Girls, what you doing? Stop! Stop what y'all doing? I'm your auntie!" Meashell shouted.

"Yes and you're the auntie that left us for dead." Kaia said as her and Lina moved closer with the hot hatchet in their hand. They pressed the axe against the left side of Meashell cheeks.

"Ahhhhhh!" Meashell screamed while bouncing her leg up and down.

"No girls, higher like y'all did with the man," Faith said.

Meashell started to panic, as they pulled away the hatchet from her burnt cheek, and the henchmen reheated it. "Any higher they'll burn my eye," Meashell said.

"That's the point an eye for an eye, you took something from them and you took something from me, so we gonna take something that you gonna miss a whole lot," Faith said.

"But you killed their family, my brother and their mother!" Meashell shouted and look at her nieces, "She did it, she killed the whole village," Meashell said.

"Because of you auntie, because of you," Kaia and Lina said at the same time then pressed the flat part of the hatchet on to Meashell's left eye, it sizzled and popped then burned, a weird smell lingered in the air. "Ahhhhh! Aghhh!" Meashell screamed in excruciating pain even after the girls removed the hatchet.

"Y'all did good girls, here eat a gummy and go back to training," Faith said handing them a gummy each and a henchmen escorted them out the room.

"Shit if they eat that gummy it's fuck training. They're going to go to sleep or bouncing off the wall, you're not supposed to give kids edibles," Jainice said.

Faith shrugged her shoulder, "I'm still learning but these training kids to be henchmen is way better than my fathers' idea, training grown ass men, train kids and all they know is us," Faith said.

"Doing both would be smart." Jainice replied.

Meashell stopped screaming and couldn't believe they was having a conversation as if everything that was happening was normal. "Ugh!" she groaned in pain. Her face stung and burned at the same time, she couldn't see out her left eye, not knowing if it was burned closed or burned out and completely gone all the way.

"Faith ate one more gummy and passed the rest to Jainice.

"Bitch you only saved me one and a half, we gonna need more," Jainice said after she ate the gummy.

"Hell no, I'm not eating them no more after today, shit got me floating. Now let's go finish playing with your hating ass ex friend," Faith said.

"That was your henchmen, shit." Jainice replied.

"Is this a game to y'all, hurting people?" Meashell said.

"Not people, but you, yes," Jainice responded.

"When did you turn into her, and think this is okay? This isn't how the normal world works. This isn't okay torturing and killing people while you high." Meashell shouted and her face hurt, felt as it was peeling.

"Who said anything about killing you, we gonna keep you alive for a long time," Faith said and walked over to the two other chairs and pulled down the sheets and let them drop to the floor. Meashell turned her head and looked, it was Fabio with a gag ball in his mouth, he was in and out of consciousness, opening his eyes then going back to sleep, then she looked at his arms and legs they was missing, and burned closed where they should be. We have to let the air hit the wounds for the first week before wrapping it," Faith said. Then next to Fabio was Doctor Rashi with a pink gag ball in his mouth and his limbs had been chopped off as well and he was fast asleep snoring. "They're both on morphine, you don't feel no pain and sleep like a baby," Faith said and walked behind he.

"What the fuck is this? Why would you do such a thing to people? Just kill them already this is inhumane? Why would you do this, I don't understand?" Meashell said looking at Fabio with her good eye. She could hear a cage or two open behind her and clicking sounds as Faith walked toward her then came in front of her with a leash in each hand, she handed Jainice a leash.

It took Meashell a second to realize what she was staring at, she recognized Jason right away. He was standing on all four limbs with a hard plastic around them to help him put pressure on them. He had a spiked collar around his neck and a gag ball in his mouth, on the second leash was an older heavy set woman with her hair shaved off bald a sad look in her eyes as she stood on all fours with a red gag ball in her mouth. "I'm not gonna kill you Meashell you're gonna be a part of my zoo, I'm gonna keep you alive for years to come, so I can remember the lesson you taught me, just like Jason here, my baby daddy will never leave my side for crossing me. Now would you baby? Faith said and removed his gag ball strap and he made a weird sound as he tried to talk, sounding like an animal calling for help. "Oh did I forget to mention I cut their tongue out and popped one eardrum; it keeps them from talking straight and kinda threw them off balance, but it works. I leave one ear untouched so they can hear me when I give orders and talk to them, venting about my day, like today. Today was a very bad day for me, I lost a trusted friend but thanks to Jainice and her gummy's I'm okay," Faith said then handed her lease to a henchmen and Jainice did the same. They took Jason and Regina back to their cages.

Meashell felt as if her heart was gonna stop at any moment. The thought of her being stuck like that forever planted in her mind, unable to speak, unable to really move, no longer having hands or feet. "You bitches are crazy as hell, fucking no I won't let you do that me. No I rather die!" Meashell shouted.

"Well there's nothing you can do sweetie. You're gonna be one of Faith's pets, don't worry the pets in the zoo eat well," Jainice said as a henchmen passed her the double blade axe.

"Yea, but I'm thinking we should start removing all her teeth, I did it with Jason he tried to bite me once the other day," Faith said while smiling and spinning in a circle.

Jainice raise the axe to swing, "I always wanted to try this, it freaked me out the first two times but after watching her do it so many times, you kinda get use to it, like it's normal. I wanted to know how it feels when the blade slices through flesh one time," Jainice said while laughing then put down the axe and grabbed her chest. "These damn edibles got me tripping, she turned around and said to Faith.

Meashell used all her strength and broke the leather strap that started as a little rip. She quickly unstrapped her next hand then legs, a henchmen rushed her and she spin kicked him in the face that grabbed the i.v pole that was hooked up to Fabio and kick up the mask of the henchmen and jammed the pole into his neck, a henchmen tried to grab her from behind, she kicked him in the stomach and ran over to the dead henchmen and grab his knife out of his holster.

She looked and seen the nurse in pink scrubs standing over by the side of the wall and ran over to her and stabbed her five times in the stomach, the nurse screamed then slid down the wall in slow motion while holding her stomach as five more henchmen rushed in the room, "I'm not letting you do that to me, you're crazy. I'll kill you all," Meashell said as two more henchmen rushed her at the same time, she kick one in the balls, he bent over to grab his dick and she stab him in the back of the head. The next one grabbed her from the side locking his arms around her as another one came charging at her, she front kicked the one charging toward her in the face and stabbed the one that had her in the bear hug in his arms and then jammed the knife in his neck. He backpedaled holding his neck and fell sideways.

Meashell held the knife out, pointing at the air, "I dare one of you to get close, come on! Who next?" she said hoping she could buy time to catch her breath. "Why am I so tired, I normally can take out more men than this before feeling tired but being in that cage got me weak. No exercising just sleeping and eating, my body don't feel right, it's sluggish for some reason. If I can't beat them all I just got to get Faith or Jainice to kill me. The henchmen won't they're gonna try and catch me alive, I refuse to be one of those pets. Hell no, imagine living your life like that just waiting for death but it never comes. To be walked around like a dog? To have no tongue to talk. I'm already blind in one eye, I should've killed my nieces in the jungle myself and left their little bodies for the hyenas but now isn't the time for should've or could've. I need a fucking plan. The more henchmen I kill the more keep coming but I killed the nurse hmmm." Meashell said to herself. "Stop, I'll give y'all information if you promise that one of you will fight me and kill me or die trying, either way I go out like I want to." Meashell said. Her back was against the wall next to the dead nurse and three dead henchmen as five more stood in front of her ready to attack looking for an opening.

Faith was still spinning in a circle high as hell and Jainice laughing. Faith stopped spinning and felt as if she would hit the floor, "Okay what information you can tell me that's gonna stop me from choosing to fuck you up?" Faith asked.

"First, you got to promise that you won't chop me up and you'll fight me and kill me, if I beat you or Jainice y'all got to let me go." Meashell said.

"Sure, I promise I won't chop you up," Faith said smiling.

"Why you smiling like that, like you're lying? Meashell asked.

"Naw she will keep her promise, I'll make sure she does, and you know for a fact I kept my promise," Jainice said.

Meashell looked at Jainice and knew she would keep her word, all the years they've been friends, if Jainice said she was gonna do something for you she would, if she promised, she kept it, even if it put her out her way. "Okay we have a deal," Meashell said and the henchmen backed up just a little.

"I know where Minglee went but it's gonna be hard for y'all to get her, my stupid ass should've went with her but thought I'd be good in my old village. I really don't like Minglee like that, she's bossy, I guess because she's so short but she always acted like she suppose to be giving orders and everyone suppose to follow or like she's so gangster. In reality, she's soft as hell and a bitch but since the training her head has gotten even bigger, thinking she could beat anyone. I just couldn't bear to be around her any longer," Meashell said.

"Get to the point, you're boring me and bringing down my high and I don't think Jainice have any more gummies." Faith said rolling her eyes.

"Psst," Meashell sucked her teeth, the point I was making is I couldn't follow Minglee, she was too bossy anyway where you'll find her is in Africa." Meashell said.

Africa is big, what part? Faith asked.

"Logo Nigeria. You won't be able to get to her easy, with the skills she learned from the compound she will be a queen over there. All she has to do was take over a militia, their full of killers even children armed with Ak47's but if Minglee started training them in the henchmen ways, she would have an army and your hyenas won't work over there. Where you think your father gets the hyenas from then breed them… Africa. They know how to handle them since they catch and sell them. Going over there is gonna be a big issue for you, no cake walk like my village." Meashell said.

Faith sat down on the floor and let Meashell words roll around her head, "I'll figure it out okay, chop her up now." Faith said than laid on the floor.

"Wait! Jainice you promised, you always keep your promise," Meashell replied.

"And I still am, I promised Faith won't chop you up, I never said I wouldn't, so the promise is kept sweetie," Jainice said then looked at the henchmen. "Grab her please and thank you, Jainice said to the henchmen.

"No! Fuck no Meashell shouted as a henchmen rushed her, she side kicked him, making him fall on to his ass and the next one ran straight at her and she stabbed him in the left eye, the one on the floor she ran up to him and pulled his head back and sliced his neck wide opened.

"Hah hah ha!" Faith bust out laughing while laying sideways on the floor with her head in her hands, watching everything and felt as if the room was spinning in slow motion.

"Kill me! Kill me!" Meashell shouted and ran pass two henchmen and attacked Jainice. Swinging the knife wildly, Jainice back stepped and moved side to side to avoid getting stabbed, Meashell didn't see the henchmen sneaking on her left side because of her new burned eye, it left a new blind spot for people to walk on. She felt a hard hit to the back of her head, knocking her to the ground. A henchmen grabbed her legs while the one that hit her on the head with a baton tried to grab the knife out her hand. Meashell twisted around onto her back and stab him in the chin, he grabbed his chin to stop the bleeding and Meashell snatched the baton out his hand and hit him on the head with it, then start swinging it at the henchmen holding her feet, he backed up and let go of her leg and she kick him with all her strength, his back slammed into the wall and she jumped up and started beating him with the baton like he'd stolen something, hitting him in the head repeatedly until his mask flew off and then kept hitting him on the side of his head, it cracked and dented, like when you hit a boiled egg with a spoon over and over and watch it dent up. He coughed up blood and slouched over and stopped breathing.

Meashell stood up straight to see Jainice still holding the axe smiling and Faith on the floor grinning as if she was watching a movie. "What the fuck is wrong with y'all, you really found where you belong Jainice, that bitch like your sister now?" Meashell said.

"It's a shame you had to cross me, look at your work. It's beautiful, you killed six henchmen and one nurse and you only got one fucking good eye. Two years of training and now you harder than the men and look at you, you're a fucking weapon, you killed a guy with an i.v stand." Faith said still clapping, then put her head back in her hand.

"I can do this all day, keep sending them," Meashell said as four more henchmen entered the room.

"You really don't think you have the upper hand do you?" Faith asked.

"Why not, you keep sending them I'll keep killing them," Meashell said and Jainice and Faith bust out laughing.

"I told you, I won, you owe me $100 and you buying the gummy next time," Jainice said.

"What? What's so funny?" Meashell asked.

"Well for starters, the loose screw in your cage, Jainice loosened and we bet that you'll break free and kill a few henchmen. I said three, Jainice said four and that you'll think you did it all by yourself. Next, your good but you can't beat Jainice if you had both eyes and drinking Red Bull I trained her personally, and we know you can't beat me so either one of us could've stopped you a long time ago but I needed the entertainment after losing Cricket today. Next, the henchmen was ordered to grab you, but you already forgot their favorite toy, what is it?" Faith asked.

Meashell stood quiet. *"They been playing with me from jump, the whole time. This been nothing but a game to them, get high and watch Meashell make a fool of herself and bet on it. That all this was."* Meashell thought to herself.

"Hey, what's their favorite toy?" Faith asked again. Meashell looked pass the four henchmen as she gripped the baton in one hand and the knife in the next.

"The dart gun," Meashell replied. Meashell looked at Faith then Jainice, "Fuck you both, I rather die!" she shouted then stabbed herself in the stomach three times. "Dart her now!" she could hear Faith scream. Meashell then ran the knife across her right wrist and fell to the ground on her ass. Laughing, "I got the last laugh. Hahah I got the last laugh bitches, the jokes on you, I win." Meashell said as a dart hit her in the center of her chest and she fought to keep her eyes opened, they kept closing. When she open them she could see Jainice walking toward her, she closed them again and opened them and Jainice was now standing over her with the axe. She close them once more then opened them to see Jainice swinging the axe at her right arm then she passed out losing consciousness. Meashell could see the bright white light, it shined so bright she could see. "I guess it's true, it's like the movies you go into the light and it's all over, and that means I'm going to heaven,"

Meashell said out loud to herself. Than could hear a woman voice and beeping.

"Her heart rate 111 and blood pressure a little high at 149/100 but she will be okay."

Meashell tried to see out both her eyes but couldn't, she was able to get her right eye open. "What's going on? Is this heaven, I made it to heaven," Meashell said in a weak voice. "I get to meet God and Pop Smoke," Meashell said. "Why can't I move or see?" Meashell mumbled.

"If there is a heaven you'll never make it there, you'll be going to hell with the rest of us, beside we would have more fun there, who wants to be somewhere you can't kill no one or eat gummies and get high?" Meashell heard a voice say and her heart started beating fast. Then the bright light was moved out her face. She lifted her head up to look around. "Here let me help you." she heard Jainice over her head then as if magic it felt as if she was push up right and was now standing up.

Meashell looked down to see she was on a steel table and was pushed up and she looked around to see the room she was in was green and a nurse wearing blue scrubs was looking at the heart monitor and checking her vitals. She could feel an i.v in her neck. "Wait what going on? This isn't heaven," Meashell said.

"No bitch it's more like hell on earth, see you thought you could pull a fast one. Your last move was smart, I give you that but you forgot a few things, like we have our own medical center in each compound with a nurse and doctor staff," Faith said while smiling her evil grin.

"But I sliced my wrist there was no way," Meashell said then looked at her right arm and it was gone. "My arm! My arm! What you do to my arm?" Meashell screamed while crying and looking at what was left of her arm.

"Yea that was smart but Jainice just chop the arm off and burned your wound before you bled to death, then we had the doctor work on your stomach. Shocking you didn't hit no major organs, even I was surprised about that one. Shit stabbing people in the right spot was part of your training, so either you wasn't paying attention or you didn't really want to kill yourself. So it's a win, win for me bitch." Faith stopped talking as Lefty entered the room.

"Mistress, I have good news and I have great news," Lefty said holding an iPad.

"Give me the good news first," Faith said. Lefty passed her the iPad.

"We found your brother, the oldest is thirty one his name is Michael and the youngest is eleven and his name is mike they live in Long Island New York with a woman named Envy, your brother's wife and another baby." Lefty said knowing they can revenge Cricket's death.

Faith stare at Michael's picture with hate, "Get the men ready." Faith ordered.

"Wait before we do that you need to hear the great news, keep scrolling right," Lefty said. Faith eyes opened up wide as pictures of Antonio and Sabrina popped up pushing a stroller and walking like they didn't have a care in the world. "We found your baby, Sabrina and Antonio, they're in Miami, living in a suburban but we don't know for how long. Sabrina's trying to get plastic surgery in the states this time, we think once she does, they'll be on the move again," Lefty said.

Faith looked at the screen in a daze, staring at the baby stroller. "My baby," Faith said while crying. "We will leave right away," Faith said.

"Yes Mistress, I have henchmen in plain clothes down there now, blending in and watching Antonio and Sabrina's every move." Lefty replied.

Faith hugged him tightly. "I love you my friend, this really made my day," Faith said while crying tears of joy.

"You know I got your back until they take me under." Lefty replied as she broke their embrace. She look back at Jainice who was smiling for her, standing behind Meashell's table.

"Make it fast, we got to go get your god child," Faith said.

Meashell breathe a sigh of relief. *"If she's chasing after her brother and baby, I'll get one more day to live and try to escape."* Meashell thought to herself then looked at Jainice walk around the table holding Faith's chrome double blade axe. "I made a promise and got to keep it, I promised she wouldn't," Jainice said.

"Wait no! Y'all don't have time for this! Just go!" Meashell shouted.

"Oh we got time for traitor trifling ass hoes like you." Jainice said then swung, chopping of Meashell left leg under the knee. "Ahhhh!" Meashell hollered in agonizing pain.

Faith look up then looked back at the picture of Sabrina and Antonio. "You cut too low, you got to cut above the knee, or she won't be able to walk on all fours properly," Faith said in a notch's tone.

"Yea you're right my bad, this double blade axe is surprisingly light as hell, I have to hold back my strength so I don't cut through the steel table, it's already a slice mark in it now, do we get these on wholesale or what?" Jainice said.

"Yea, that's the way my father made it, to be light so I can swing without getting tired, and I have no idea about the table that's Lefty's job. Hurry up before she bleed to death," Faith said.

"Oh yea right," Jan said and swung again, cutting off the little piece she missed as a henchmen put the blow torch on the axe and Jainice screwed up her face while placing it on Meashell's left leg. "Ewww, that shit nasty, how you kept doing it all the time, human flesh smells like burnt pork and her skin sticks to the damn axe," Jainice said.

"You get use to it; the more you do something it becomes routine. You think I had a girl or a boy? I keep staring at this picture but I can't tell, they have a black stroller, so I can't go off colors because they have no style. Shit, they was like that before all of this but I really want to know what my baby is." Faith said in a sad tone.

Jainice stopped what she was doing and walked over to her and hugged her. "Don't worry, the hard part over with, we found them. Now we know where they are, we will get your baby back and the best part of this is they won't see us coming. They think you're dead. Just like that bitch over there did," Jainice said pointing at Meashell screaming and crying, with one arm and leg missing. Jainice kissed Faith's forehead, "What started out as a terrible day turned into something great, Cricket's looking out for you," Jainice said then walked away.

"I guess you're right," Faith said and stopped looking at the pictures on the iPad.

"Anyway, what made you choose an axe as your weapon and the hatchets and ain't hatchets nothing but mini axe?" Jainice asked.

"You still high, ain't you? Faith asked.

"Yea, just a little." Jainice said and swung, chopping off Meashell's left arm.

"Ahh, please stop! Just stop! Kill me!" Meashell begged while crying.

"You did it again, I'm starting to think you're doing it on purpose, your aim not that bad, I seen you shoot remember." Faith said.

"Maybe I am." Jainice replied while smiling then looked at Meashell. "I cut under the elbow again. It's supposed to be above. You stay still,"

Jainice said then swung, chopping the little piece off. Then the henchmen heated up the axe with the blow torch and Jainice placed it onto Meashell's open wound burning it closed.

"I didn't pick it, the hatchets picked me, it felt right in my hand, better than the knife. Just chopping felt good and yes a hatchet is a mini axe, but the double blade axe is something different something the Vikings use to use, I like it. You don't? Faith asked.

"No, it don't feel right in my hands, I think I like a long knife, the daggers better; and why they just didn't call hatchets small axe instead?" Jainice asked.

"Girl shut up and finish. Every time you get to high you gotta start sounding like a philosopher or ask crazy questions, like why water wet," Faith said and roll her eyes.

"Please stop, no more! I can't take no more sister," Meashell begged.

"Oh now I'm your sister, I wasn't when you jumped and left me for dead," Jainice said and swung again and chopped off Meashell's right leg and watched her scream and cry while the henchmen heated up the axe, she then pressed it against her skin. "I don't like this shit, the meat and skin smell funny after you burn it. I won't be doing this again that's for sure. The smell makes my stomach bubble up, it don't bother you?" Jainice asked.

"No and sometimes I hold my breath until I finish up and take her tongue, she's the only one that hasn't passed out.

"Men are pussies if they had to give birth the world wouldn't be populate, they don't know pain, like getting your cycle every month, the cramps, they would die. But do I really have to take her tongue? My high wearing off and this stuff starting to freak me out, it might be good if she could talk shit back," Jainice said and Faith raised her right eyebrow and folded her arms and just looked at her. "Okay," Jainice said as a nurse passed her a long chrome needle that looked like an ice pick.

"Stop please don't do this to me, just kill me please," Meashell said weakly.

Jainice held her face and pushed the needle in deep into her left eye until blood poured out mixed with wax, "You don't need that side any way no more, face all burnt, eyeball gone and popped, might as well be blind and deaf on the same side," Jainice said as Faith passed her a knife and a henchmen squeezed Meashell's cheeks forcing her mouth opened.

"Nooo, Jainice no! Kill me! You was my friend, don't do this to me!" Meashell said while crying uncontrollably. Jainice grabbed her tongue.

"I was your friend and still would have been, even if you ran and left me but I can never forgive you for beating on me and jumping me when I was weak, that friendship shit is dead, you showed me that." Jainice said as she sawed off Meashell's tongue then threw it on the floor. "Now welcome to the zoo!" Jainice said and walked away with Faith. Leaving Meashell crying with thick red blood mixed with saliva dripping out her mouth.

Chapter 7

Jainice sat in the zoo room watching the pets eat, Meashell just laid on the floor in her cage watching Regina and Fabio as he was eating the corn and rice with gravy happily.

Jainice pulled out her blunt and lit, and heard the door open behind her and Faith walked in and sat on the black velvet couch next to her, "I knew I'd find you in here," Faith said as Jainice passed the blunt to her.

"So are we ready to leave? It's been two days since you got the information now," Jainice said.

"Yea, I had to get some things ready. Sabrina is smart, I played chess with her, rushing in is only gonna backfire on me." Faith replied.

"You ever been to an aquarium?" Jainice asked.

"No," Faith hit the blunt a few times and passed it back.

"Well after this, we should go and take your baby, you'll like it. It's kinda like this, looking at your pets. Plus, it's relaxing as hell when high." Jainice responded.

"Everything relaxing as hell to you when you're high," Faith said causing each other to laugh. "But to be on a serious note, what if I'm not a good parent and I end up being like her?" Faith said looking at Regina in the cage eating.

"Naw, you can't be like her because you know what it felt like to be treated bad and you not gonna do the same thing to your child, it would fuck with your head," Jainice said talking with smoke in her lungs and mouth holding it in.

"You always say the right shit my friend," Faith said.

"I know that why people love me, but off topic I think Lefty gay. Well I been thought so and it's no big deal. I always wanted a gay male friend but he give too many tale tale signs." Jainice said.

"Yea, I been thought as much, to each its own. Any way I got something for you," Faith said and turned around and a henchmen came in the room with a small beige case and passed it to Faith then left. Faith looked at the big case then passed it to Jainice. "It is a case like the one that saved our lives, but I wanted to gift you something.

"Is it weed, tell me it's weed. I heard they got some new shit out that taste like fruity pebbles," Jainice said.

"Psst, be serious," Faith said.

"Bitch, I am serious. I can taste that weed now in my head," Jainice said while smiling then opening the case and smiled. It was a black cat like suit, a metal rod that looked like a baton and a wide black bracelet. I had them made. They checked the old compound that collapsed, and they found scraps of the rare metal that my axe and suit is made of, it's called Teflon. I had a suit made for you. Thank God you're slim-thick, it was just enough melt for it. It's pretty much indestructible unless you got Teflon weapons." Faith said.

"But we heal?" Jainice whispered.

"Yea, but that's not always gonna be enough, look what happened to J-Money or the gun my brother used, my father said don't even let people know we can do that, not our enemies, it give us an advantage over them. Element of surprise and makes us a whole lot scarier," Faith said then picked up the black bracelet and put it in Jainice's right arm and took the blunt from her. "Pick up the metal rod." Faith said.

Jainice picked it up. "Hmm it's not too light or too heavy what is it? I'm supposed to beat people with it? That shit would be fun?" Jainice said swinging as if she was hitting someone in the head with it.

Faith rolled her eyes. "Sometimes I wonder about you. Press the button on the side." Faith said.

"This one," Jainice pressed a button and a wide short blade popped out. "Oh this shit hot, it's a dagger But how the blade fit in there and why is it so wide?" Jainice said looking at it in amazement and poking the air and realized the metal rod was a handle.

"Teflon metal is one of the rarest and strongest metals used only by this group of females assassins and it made them the most deadliest killers my father has seen, I noticed when my brother tried to blow off my face, I turned my hatchet sideways to the flat side, the bullet hit it, and it stopped it. The shit pushed me back and made my arm vibrate for ten minutes afterwards but it stopped the bullet.

"So that's why your dagger is wide, just in case. Now press the button on the other side," Faith said.

"Bitch there's more!" Jainice smiled and pressed the button and a blade popped out on the other end, she held the handle and looked at the double blade dagger, and stood up and started swinging, acting as if she was fighting. "So I can stab a motherfucker with one end and pull it out of him and stab another asshole real fast with the other end." Jainice said.

"How does it feel?" Faith asked.

"More like me, like your axe and hatchets. I like stabbing or poking a motherfucker up. It's the Harlem girl in me," Jainice said.

"Throw it at the wall." Faith ordered. Jainice turned away from the cages and threw the double blade dagger and it slammed into the wall. "Now open the palm of your hand," Faith said. Jainice looked at her like she was stupid but did it anyway. The double blade dagger flew back into her hand.

"Holy shit, how it do that?" Jainice asked.

"The bracelet is a powerful magnet and its magnets in the dagger, when you throw it the magnet can push it faster or harder and when you flex your wrist a certain way it calls the blade back, fucking technology, it's crazy. The bracelet is for when you're not wearing your suit, your suit has it built in already." Faith said while smoking looking at Meashell just lay there and her mother Regina stared at her with hate in her eyes. "You keep looking at me like that bitch, I'll take your eyes. How would you like that, deaf in one ear and no eyesight. That should be fun, won't it?" Faith said and Regina's face twisted up with anger but she looked down and away, knowing Faith would do it.

"Can your stuff do this too?" Jainice asked and came over to her and grabbed the blunt.

"Yea." Faith replied changing her mood looking at Regina once more.

"And you never told me or showed anyone?" Jainice asked.

"I try with them in private, learning how to use it, again you can't over use something too much then people would know and that takes the surprise out of it when you kill them, less people know what you're fully capable of. They will underestimate you and that's what you want, shit the only people that know what your dagger can do is me and you," Faith said.

"What about the guys who built it?" Jainice asked.

"Oh I fed two of them to Raven and Egypt and the other two to the hyenas when they was done and kept their files on it. The henchmen don't even know about my weapons or suit or yours. That's how it should be." Faith said.

"Damn bitch, that was overkill, what if it breaks or we want to make another one?" Jainice asked and passed her back the blunt.

"It won't break and that way I kept their files down to a flash drive, we can easily kidnap someone to build another one." Faith said.

"So what you gonna do about her, she haven't ate in two days? Think she trying to starve herself to death," Jainice said.

That's not gonna work. Regina tried that shit the first few days as well, watch," Faith said and got up and went to the room door and talked to a henchmen then came back and sat down. A few seconds later two henchmen entered the room holding some stuff Jainice couldn't make out what it was. They opened the cage Meashell was in, she was in a black t-shirt and a big pink pamper, they dragged her out the cage, she didn't put up no fight. Jainice looked into her eye, it was as if she giving up all hope and was stuck in depression. One of the henchmen forced her mouth open and pulled out a syringe and injected her cheek with it and grabbed pliers and started yanking out her front teeth.

"Oh damn," Jainice said.

"Naw, it look worse than it is, they shot her up with Novocain, her shit's completely numb, they're only gonna take her front teeth." Faith said.

"I don't care what you say, getting teeth pulled hurt and why she look like that?" Jainice asked.

"They all look like that the first month or so, besides Fabio over there, he give no fucks, as long as I feed him good, he's happy. It's so weird," Faith said while laughing but the rest get depressed, suicidal and when they realize they can't kill themselves and that this is life for them, they accept it. They start eating and moving around, even watch the tv I leave on for them," Faith said Jainice watched the henchmen pull out all Meashell's front teeth then place a red funnel in her mouth, they push the small end down her throat, and picked up a jug and started pouring.

"What is that in the jug. They are pouring that down her throat, what are they doing?" Jainice asked.

"They feeding her Pediasure and later oatmeal, it will keep her weight up, they'll do it four times a day, and after a while they get tired of the shit and start eating on their own, it always work." Jainice looked at Meashell and started to feel bad for her, *"Maybe death would've been better."* Jainice thought to herself. As more food was forced down Meashell's throat, a look in her eyes was as if her soul left her body.

Chapter 8

Weston Florida was an upper class neighborhood, made for the rich only, most people lived there because it was a twenty minute drive to Miami. Heavenly Gates, was a gated community, it was full of million dollar homes. If you didn't own a house or was on a guest list, you couldn't get passed the front gate. Faith and Jainice watched as luxury cars went in and out the gated community.

"Waiting for them to leave isn't a good plan, we been here two days. They never have to leave, the fucking community has its own grocery stores and movie theater, not to mention two five star restaurants, an indoor swimming pool and gym," Jainice said as her and Faith sat in the back of a Mercedes Benz and Lefty in the driver seat.

"We're gonna have to rush the neighborhood and house, and try to get my baby in time before the police come," Faith said and looked at the front gate.

"I'm tired of looking like an old ass lady, I'm ready to look like myself or younger, this some bullshit!" Sabrina shouted while sitting in the backyard by the pool and looking at her black medium size yacht parked in the back of her house.

A river ran through the backyard on their side of the streets. People would drive there yacht through the river into Miami's ocean and party, drink, and ride jet skis.

"It's easier said than done, I'm still waiting for my doctor friends to forge the birth certificates, once that happens we can go anywhere in the world you like, back to Dominican Republic to get your body and face done but I think you can still get a good job done here," Antonio said while drinking a glass of Hennessy, with his gun holster strapped on his shoulders.

"I really don't like their work but I'll let them start on my body and face next week, because I can't go another day looking like this, and being in Miami don't help with all these beautiful people with beautiful bodies and me stuck looking like an old hag." Sabrina replied.

"You know why we picked Miami from here we can be in any Caribbean Island fast if we ever need to escape. Honestly, I want to get to Jamaica and live our lives there and never look back. I can be a doctor, open up a clinic and we can open up a small hotel as well," Antonio said.

"I bet you would like that, want to be anywhere they don't wear clothes or walking around in swimsuits," Sabrina said with an attitude.

"Please don't start again, I am about to grill you some chicken, just relax and have you checked on the nanny?" Antonio replied.

"Yea, I check on her nasty ass. I forgot what hard work it is to raise a baby when they that little, it's so much better when they can use the bathroom on their own and put food in the microwave, and don't try to shut me up with food but it will work," Sabrina said while sipping red wine.

"You barely do anything, what you mean hard work?" Antonio said.

"See there you go about to put yourself back in the damn dog house, when you was about to get out of it but got to run your smart ass mouth. I do a lot, I had to mop floors and clean blood and kiss ass for two years just so we can get our revenge on a bitch you stuck your dick in. You want me to get started Antonio because I will. I haven't forgave you and never will but you're part of my next plan, that's it, our children are dead because of you, so don't act as if I don't put work in. Without me, you would've never found that chocolate hoe, and to be honest the things I seen you couldn't handle. That place still give me nightmares and I haven't found my friend Maria since we got there." Sabrina shouted.

"Okay! Okay, I was just saying the nanny does a lot of the work that's all." Antonio replied.

"And let me guess, you want to fuck the nanny as well, go head stick your dick in her let's see if you found another crazy ass bitch." Sabrina replied.

"You know what, I'm sorry," Antonio said then left and went into the kitchen and came back out with a blow of seasoned chicken and put it on the grill, he lit up a cigar and put on his brown chef apron.

Sabrina stood there sitting in her lounge chair with her leg shaking staring into pool water, day dreaming. She lit a cigarette, "Are the men in place?" she asked while her left leg shook uncontrollably up and down as she started to overthink.

"Yea, I told you I rented two homes in this neighborhood, they are full of our soldiers, I don't think we really need that much men in the area, look where we at? Nothing can happen out here," Antonio said.

Sabrina looked at him, "To be so smart you're stupid as hell, nice neighborhoods is where all the crazy shit happens and real killers live, look at us. Plus, you don't know Black Ice. I don't think he's human, if he wants in this neighborhood nothing could stop him, not ever our men." Sabrina replied.

"You remember what we did to those henchmen and his men?" Antonio said proudly.

"Don't let your ego give you a big head, that wasn't Black Ice men, those was that little girls' you was fucking, she only had twenty men there and she was pregnant. Her father is a worse animal, a beast in the night; that man scares the shit out of me literally, if he ever finds out I'm alive he will come for us. He use to look at me as if he didn't know if he wanted to spit on me or chop off my head, he didn't trust me one bit. I think he just wanted to see what I was up too," Sabrina said.

"Fuck him, if he comes I'll kill him like we killed his hoe ass daughter. They're only human with sick minds, from what you tell me they just get off by doing sick shit. If anyone tries to hurt you they'll die, that's all to it. Now enough with all these negative vibes it's blowing my high and the chicken almost done." Antonio said.

Sabrina sat there just thinking, *"He don't understand, we got lucky that day, he got lucky that day, his ego don't get it. We killed a pregnant woman she was weak at the time, and her father is a different type of monster, but that's why I got to think ahead and be the brains, can't depend on him at all. The investment into the bitcoins is paying off. I own 300 of them and the price of each coin is now hundred thousand, if the price keep going up I'll be able to hide from Black Ice forever and hire a better missionary with even better killers to protect me."* Sabrina thought to herself. Her train of thought was broken when she heard Antonio say, "Hey baby the chicken done, it's on the kitchen table. I'll be back gonna check on the guys," Antonio said then walked out the front door. The sun was just going down making the sky a dull orange color, he walked across the street to a house similar to his and knocked on the door three times. The door opened and a Caucasian man wearing a pink button up shirt with the matching shorts on opened the door, "Ralph," Antonio said as he entered. The inside was nothing like the outside, there was men everywhere some dressed in camouflage uniforms others in casual clothes, all with guns, walking around talking and eating. The living room had a few desks set up with computer monitors and people sitting at them.

"Any update?" Antonio asked.

"No, it's been the same for the last three months, nothing, just rich people buying stuff, and jogging. All the same shit, kinda boring if you ask me. My men need to stretch their legs, when are we moving to a different Country?" Ralph asked.

"Soon, I hope by two more weeks. I'm tired of being here too, just waiting on one more birth certificate and then we can go to Jamaica or The British Virgin Islands , and y'all can be out in the open, as of now it's too many of y'all, y'all scare these white people. No offense Ralph." Antonio said.

"Sounds like a plan, the other house down the block doing well. We have the men taking turns going out and about to the city, to relax a little and do recon, as of now you paying us for nothing. I don't mind the free paycheck, It's just the freedom is killing us, no exercising and training making us feel slow, that's all." Ralph replied.

"Yea, yea, it is what it is. We all got to bare things we don't like, for me it's my wife, and she scared of the Black Ice guy, but I think we killed his ass too when we blew up that building but anything to make her feel safe. She over there scared as hell of some fake boogie man. No one can fuck with us, we handled those fake ass henchmen like nothing and we can do it any time, so take the free paycheck for now," Antonio said while walking through the living to the back door.

"You're heading over to Miss Marcy house?" Ralph asked.

"You're in my business and I don't like that," Antonio said with a smile on his face as he walked out the back door and passed the pool and hopped the black fence into the next yard, then hopped another fence until he was two blocks from home in an elegant backyard. He could see Miss Marcy in the pool, laying on a floating bed while smoking from her vape pen, she looked up and smile when she saw him. Antonio's dick got hard with the sight of her, she was thick with no stomach and a nice ass, he was sure she paid for it, her body was perfect and looked like she went and got it done more than once. Her double D breast was full and standing up at attention. Her honey complexion seemed to glow. "Hey baby," she said in a thick Colombian accent. That turned Antonio on even more.

"Did you get my gift I had mailed to your house?" Antonio asked.

"Yes, I got the shoes and the diamond bracelet daddy," Miss Marcy said and climbed out the pool with nothing on but her royal blue bikini and went to Antonio arms, he squeeze her ass while they kissed. Then broke their embrace as his dick fought to break through his jeans.

"How much time we have tonight before your husband come home?" Antonio asked.

"After selling cars all day, knowing him, he'll be in Miami in some Cuban club all night and fucking with other women and won't come home until sometime tomorrow afternoon with a weak excuse why, like I'm dumb. So to answer your question you can spend the night daddy. I miss this dick," Miss Marcy said and grabbed his dick.

Sabrina grabbed a plate and put a few pieces of grilled chicken on it, then went upstairs to check on the nanny, she was on her job. She smiled and went back downstairs and out the front door and across the street, and knocked on the door, Ralph opened the door, and she walked passed him straight into the living with Ralph following behind her. "So he's at his bitch spot again? Pull up surveillance," Sabrina asked the men in the living room in front of the computer monitors, they pulled up the live camera feed showing Antonio in Miss Marcy's backyard kissing. Sabrina bit into one of the chicken wings and passed one to Ralph, then one to the man on the computer monitor. "You'd think after getting his family murdered he'd stop this shit, but look at him, haven't learned a fucking thing, just slow in the head. The only thing different is, it's actually a woman close to his age. Now what if that woman man find out and want to kill him and me? He's so slow, I swear, and still haven't figured out I know and been paying y'all double to really work for me." Sabrina said while rolling her eyes and eating the chicken. "At least his stupid ass can grill some good chicken." Sabrina said.

"He really can," Ralph said and Sabrina looked at him as if she wanted the smack him.

She rolled her eyes and put the plate of chicken down on the desk. "Y'all finish that and you upstairs and eat my ass while I think of how we gonna kill my husband when we get this next birth certificate." Sabrina said and grabbed Ralph by the hand, the other soldiers in the living room just looked at him and grabbed some chicken, as he was led upstairs holding Sabrina hand.

Faith looked at the sun go all the way down, and exhaled deeply then looked at Jainice sitting next to her, they both were dressed in their all black bodysuits with their holsters attached, and ready. "Let's do this," Faith said to Lefty as he started the Mercedes Benz and pulled out to the road and pulled up to the gated community security booth and rolled down the back window of Benz. Faith stuck her dart gun out and shot the security guard twice, then Lefty stepped out and shot the one in the booth, as six black vans with the word Amazon Delivery on them and one eighteen wheeler truck pulled up behind them. Two henchmen jumped out dressed like security guards went in the booth while the other henchmen dragged the two unconscious guards away.

"So are we gonna dart the entire neighborhood? Jainice asked.

"If we have to." Faith replied nonchalant.

"What about those damn soldiers?" Jainice asked.

"We take as many as we can and kill those we can't but no evidence must be left behind." Faith said and looked behind her to see more black vans that said Amazon Delivery just park on the street waiting for her orders. "Let's do this," Faith said while thinking about her baby. Her henchmen pressed a button and the gate opened to the community. Lefty drove in the community followed by the vans and eighteen wheeler stayed at the front. The vans went in different directions in the neighborhood. Everyone got their orders, "Keep a lookout for soldiers, Antonio or Sabrina, do not engage I repeat do not engage just report back." Lefty said into the headphone bud in his ear.

"So how we gonna find them, there's over two hundred homes in this neighborhood," Jainice said.

"Listen I'm nervous and you're not helping me friend." Faith replied.

"Why you nervous, talk to me," Jainice said.

"We're so close to getting the bitch that stole my baby and anything can go wrong and it scares me and what really scares me is what if my child don't like me, it's been gone for close to four months now, it don't know me," Faith said and held her head down.

"Don't even think like that, you got this and always have a backup plan. We will find your baby and add Antonio and Sabrina to the zoo and your child will love you, it's your blood. You love your father and he been gone out your life almost all of it but once you seen him you knew the connection, didn't you?" Jainice said.

"Yea I did." Faith replied.

"Well there you go, so stop over fucking thinking and flipping on me, you know damn well I talk a lot and ask a lot of questions when I'm high, I'm not gonna change. You should be use to it by now," Jainice said and start laughing.

Faith started laughing as well. "You do talk a lot," Lefty said as he looked at them through the review mirror as he turned the block.

"Stop!" Faith shouted and Lefty stomped the breaks.

"What! What happened?" Lefty asked nervously.

"Park the car here," Faith said with her eyes wide opened, touching her chest.

"But Mistress we're only six blocks into the neighborhood," Lefty said.

"Just do what I tell you," Faith said.

Lefty parked the car next to a huge yellow mansion that already had a few cars parked in front of it. As if a small party was taking place. "What is it?" Jainice asked.

"Remember I told you I get this weird feeling when my father sneaks up on me, I can't see him but I can feel him?" Faith asked.

"Yea and so." Jainice replied.

"Well I had that same feel when I met my brothers that night but it was different, not the same as my father, a cool chill. I could feel the little boy way long before I could see his ass. Well I have that same feeling, but it's different it's in my stomach, like a kick that happening repeatedly." Faith said.

"You sure it's not your brothers again or a different sibling that's close by?" Jainice asked.

"No, the feeling I had with the little boy was different, even with my older brother. I can't explain it but each one give off a different vibe and type of energy, my father's energy is dark, very dark, the little boy my brother is dark but the older one wasn't like me and his energy, psst I sound crazy," Faith said.

"No I believe you, people give off energy. I can meet a bitch and know I don't like her right away without her saying anything, same for a dude, I go on a date and his vibe or energy off, he could be spitting good game but something tell me don't fuck him, don't trust him and boom a day later I find out he live with his baby mother, he's broke and that wasn't his car he was driving stunting ass nigga but the point is I get it." Jainice responded.

"Well yea, kinda like that but like I said I feel something in my stomach, it's like kicking, my baby close by in one of these houses," Faith said.

"You know which one, can you stomach point it out?" Lefty looked back and asked.

"No it don't work like that. Like with my father, I know he's nearby but I never know where, same thing with my brothers I knew something wasn't

232

right, it's not a damn GPS system Lefty," Faith said.

"Well, we're between four homes two on this side and two across the street, so let's eliminate some, like the house we in front of with all these nice luxury cars. I don't think your baby would be in there because it's a full blown party and that would make a baby cry, so let's look at the house in front of us and the two across the street," Jainice said looking at Faith hold her stomach and just looking around.

"Come on give me a sign, I know you're close, I can feel you." Faith thought to herself. Then a house door opened up at the second house across the street, an old brown-skin woman wearing purple pajamas kissed a Caucasian man with muscles wearing a pink short set.

"I swear Florida people out here dress funny, they just don't give no fuck!" Lefty said.

Sabrina grabbed Ralph's dick, "We shouldn't be doing this out in the open?" Ralph said.

"Why not, all your men know already and my husband too stupid to notice anything, he think he's out smarting me, when I'm the one who put him through med school, he can't even play chess, so he'll never be a move ahead of me, no one would. Anyway I'll be back later I want my ass ate again and some dick," Sabrina said.

"You can just call the nanny or look on the camera system we have." Ralph replied.

"Naw I like to put my eyes on things, it make me feel there more secure," Sabrina said, smile and turned around and walked away. *"Even as an old woman, I still can get dick,"* Sabrina thought to herself then noticed the party next door to her house, Range Rovers, Bentleys, and a Lamborghini all was parked there, but some reason the black S-Class Mercedes Benz stuck out with her for some reason. She stare at it while walking across the street. "Hmm, why does that car not sit right with me? It's the new Benz, it's nice, probably more guest for my neighbors party. That guy always having a damn party, what it is to be young and free, no kids, no relationship, just fucking and partying. I miss my hoe days," Sabrina said as she finally crossed the street.

"Pull off, follow that bitch right there," Faith said and Lefty slowly pulled off and stopped in front of Sabrina's house.

Sabrina looked back at the black Benz while twisting her door knob, *"Now they know damn well they can't park in front of my house, I don't care how full his driveway is. If you're his guest you got to figure it out, shouldn't be throwing no damn parties every weekend any way. He lucky his house soundproof or I woulda done went to the Home Association board, I swear."* Sabrina thought to herself as she turned around and walked a few steps from her house. "Excuse me! Excuse me sweetie, you can't park here, not in front of my house," Sabrina said waving her fingers. She couldn't see inside the car because of the dark tinted windows. The back door opened. "Hell no, they about to get out and go to his party anyway." Sabrina said to herself. "If you park here I'm gonna have your car towed," Sabrina said then her heart dropped as the woman in the back seat got out.

Her long black hair touched her back, the red lipstick made her full lips even juicier, her skin complexion the color of smooth chocolate and the body suit she had on hugged every curve of her voluptuous shape. "But.. but you're dead," Sabrina said while stuttering as she looked at Faith standing there holding her stomach with her left hand. They're eyes locked and Sabrina lost control of her bowels, shitting a little bit in her underwear, and tried not to fart knowing a wet shit would escape again, her legs started shaking against each other. "But you're dead." she mumbled repeatedly.

"Hey you!" a man shouted in a deep voice. Faith turned around to see the same Caucasian man in the pink shirt with the matching shorts that was kissing Sabrina in his doorway. "You can't park there!" he shouted then looked at Sabrina's face, her body language was all wrong as if she was scared for her life or like a deer stuck looking at a car headlights before the car crashed into it. He then looked at the woman that was Faith when she turn around and looked at him. Something about her eyes screamed death. "It's a code red!" Ralph shouted just as Jainice popped out the back door and Lefty out the driver door but holding MP5 sub-machine guns with silencers on them. They squeezed the triggers to their guns before Ralph could pull his out his shorts pockets. Bullets tore through his body, his body jerked and shook and looked like he was doing a reggae dance before he hit the ground.

"Fuck what Faith said, I'm killing these assholes, they drop a building on me and I'm not giving them the chance to do it again." Jainice said.

"I'm with you on that one," Lefty said as soldiers rushed to the front door and him and Jainice continued to fire forcing them back in the house. Amazon vans rushed down the block as solider ran out a second house four houses down running to help their friends in a fight but never seen the henchmen jumping out the Amazon vans firing, sending bullets to a few of their faces and skulls.

Faith turned her head back around and look at Sabrina and Sabrina took off running to her front door and in the house, Faith grabbed the mini Ak47 out the back of the seat of the Benz and ran to the front door of Sabrina house, it was locked. She aimed at the door hinges and shot the top one off then the bottom and kicked the door in. "You took my baby! You took my babyyyyyyy!" Faith shouted while holding back tears. She scanned the house real fast, it was a double staircase as soon as you walked in. Faith ran through the living room than the kitchen, then look out the back patio door, and seen a pool and a black yacht. She looked for any moment but then could hear crying from upstairs. "My baby," Faith said to herself as she ran back to the front of the huge house and slowly made her way up the stairs and turned right. It was a long hallway with five doors and on her left was a short hallway with two bedroom doors, "I'll get right first," Faith said as she could hear a baby crying.

As she walked pass the first door it bust open and a brown-skin soldier attacked her trying to grab the mini AK47 out her hand. She kicked him in the ankle, he bent over in pain and leaned into the barrel of the gun and Faith squeezed the trigger sending ten bullets through his chest, two more soldiers ran out the room in front of her, she pulled out her hatchet and threw it. It spun through the air and slammed into one of the soldiers forehead, he dropped instantly and his body collapsed to the floor. Faith yanked her mini AK47 free of the man chest as three soldiers came out of the room behind her, holding M16 rifles. "Give me my baby!" Faith shouted looking behind her and in front of her, now surrounded in the narrow hallway. The soldiers behind her opened up fire, sending a hail of bullets in her direction, shooting her in the back, the bullets bounced off her bulletproof bodysuit but the impact made her stumble forward. The soldiers stopped firing to see her holding her side in pain.

"Yea we got the bitch, the bonus money will go to us," one of them said but looked closer and noticed there was no blood on the floor or the walls, "What the fuck!" he mumbled and stepped closer to Faith, who was hunched over in pain. Faith had dropped the mini AK47. The soldier put the barrel of his gun to the back of her head, "Why the fuck you're not bleeding?" he said.

Faith popped up and grabbed the barrel of his gun and snatched it out his hand. "She's wearing body armor aim for her…." Before he could finish the sentence Faith pulled out a knife from her holster and jam it in chin and pushed it up to his brain, she grabbed his gun and flipped around before his body hit the ground and aimed it at the other two soldiers and sent bullets into their chest and face, then ran toward the one that was behind her. He held his Glock 17 handgun and started shooting wildly, Faith use the narrow hallway to run up the walls and jumped from side to side, wall to wall like a monkey.

"What the fuck?" the soldier said and dropped his gun and dropped to his knees. "Please don't kill me," he begged as Faith now stood over him. She stretched her arm out and opened her hand, the hatchet that was jammed into one of the soldiers head yanked out of it and flew into her hand, then she swung down cracking open the skull of the soldiers head like a walnut. She yanked the hatchet out and put it back in her holster and looked at the last door down the hallway where she could hear the baby crying.

She took a deep breath then kicked the door in, the room was painted sky blue with bears painted on the wall. A light-skin young woman stood scared in the middle of the room holding a baby wrapped in a blue blanket. "Please! Please don't kill me. I'm just the nanny, don't hurt us." The light-skin woman said while holding a baby in a blue blanket.

A solider jump out from behind the door, holding a knife and swung it at Faith's face. She grabbed his wrist twisted his arm and broke it, then snapped his neck like it was nothing, he fell to the ground. Faith stepped toward her, "Give me my baby and I won't kill you, if I got to tell you again, you will die," Faith said.

The nanny slowly moved toward her and handed her the baby, Faith held the baby in her arms and removed the blanket off the baby. "It was a boy, he was light-skin complexion with Jason's face and his green eyes. Faith smiled and the weird feeling she felt when one of her family members around happened, a cool chill down her back, she turned a around to see Sabrina sneaking out the bedroom down the halls. "Where the fuck you going bitch!" Faith said through clenched teeth.

Sabrina's eyes met with Faith. "Holy shit!" she said then took off running, she pressed the bluetooth headphones in her ear.

Antonio looked at the number on his iPhone and sucked his teeth, "Hold on baby let me answer this," he said looking at Miss Marcy lay naked on the bed after they fucked, he put the phone to his ear, "Hello dear, I'm over here with the soldiers about to get drunk, what's up I need my me time with the guys. I don't like when you interrupted it," Antonio said.

"Yo shut the fuck up, I don't care that you laying up with that bitch, help me! Help me she's here! They're here and killing our men!" Sabrina shouted as she got down the stairs and ran through the living and kitchen to the patio door.

"Who here and who killing the men? I don't hear nothing." Antonio replied as he stood up out the bed.

"They're using silencers on their guns, and it's Faith she's alive, your young hoe bitch alive." Sabrina said in a panicked voice.

"That can't be, it's impossible we killed her, shot that bitch up and cut her open." Antonio replied.

"Listen she's here, you got three minutes to meet me by the river down the block or I'm leaving you," Sabrina said and ran out the back door, passed the pool and an a black gate and climbed into a yacht. She turned around to see Faith stand at the kitchen door with the baby in her left arm and a mini AK47 in her right hand, she raised it and aimed at Sabrina's back and sent a hail of bullets toward her, Sabrina started her yacht and pulled off as bullets slammed into it. Faith ran up to the yacht firing at her, but stopped when the baby started to cry from the loud noise. "I'm sorry little guy," Faith said then kiss him on the forehead. Then looked up and could see Sabrina looking back sliding down the river.

"The soldiers didn't stand a chance, being caught off guard." Jainice walked to the house front door firing then pulled out a smoke grenade and threw it in, the house filled with thick grey smoke, she strapped her Mp5 machine gun around her shoulder like a purse and looked at Lefty. Now the real fun begins," she said taking off the metal rod off her holster and pressed a button and blades popped out of both ends.

Lefty looked at her like she was crazy, "Okay, that's new but what you about to do with that?"

"You'll see or maybe you won't," Jainice said as she ran into the house. The soldiers couldn't see but was still shooting at the door, a few bullets hit Jainice suit but bounced off. She raise her forearm up to her face to protect it, as she flipped over the computer station and stabbed one of the soldiers in the back, she move around fast using the grey smoke as cover.

"It's one in here, shoot her, shoot that bitch!" one of the soldiers shouted and Jainice ran up on him and jammed her dagger into his mouth until the blade poked out the back of his head.

"Shoot this bitch." Jainice said as she yanked the dagger out and felt the impact of two bullet slamming into her back. She threw her double ended dagger behind her without looking, it spun in the air like a frisbee and slammed into a man's chest.

"Okay bitch, I see you," Lefty said as he stepped into the house with ten henchmen firing at the soldiers.

"Retreat!" one of the soldiers shouted while running toward the back door and Lefty aimed at him and blew the back of his head off. Jainice ran across the room and pulled out her dagger as a solider ran out the side door, she followed him as he cut through peoples backyard and looked back to see her gaining on him.

"Oh shit, why don't she stop, just leave me the fuck alone, go away," he shouted then fired three bullets at her, two missed but one bullet grazed the side of her cheek cutting it.

"Oh that burn, you motherfucker. I'll take you alive." Jainice said putting away her dagger and pulled out her dart gun from her thigh holster and jumped a fence after the soldier, the last fence he jump he fell into a pool and swam out of it and cut through the side of the house, he looked back and Jainice was gone.

"Thank you God," he said then turned around and Jainice was standing in front of him.

"Don't thank him yet," she said and squeeze the trigger sending a dart crashing into his skull. His body fail backwards by the side of the house and something caught Jainice eyes. "What the fuck?" she mumbled as a brown-skin older man was running with his shirt off with a M16 rifle in his hand. Jainice looked closer and smiled.

Antonio could now here the gunfire, as fast as it started it stopped, he could see Amazon vans being loaded with his soldiers bodies and henchmen cleaning up all evidence as if nothing happened, bullets shell casings was picked up, bullet holes covered up then henchmen lighting fireworks next to the neighbor house that was having a party. "What the fuck! It will look like nothing took place, just a wild party and fireworks," Antonio said to himself as he crossed the street and dropped through a neighbors backyard and ran down the river. He could see his yacht at the end of the river before it connected with the ocean, he could see Sabrina fanning him on to run faster. Then she stopped, and her eyes grew wide and the yacht started to move, "Wait! Wait, baby don't leave me!" Antonio said as he felt what felt like four big bees stings in his back, he turned around to see a slim-thick brown-skin woman smiling showing off a set of pretty teeth with a dart gun in her hand.

Antonio turned back around with his arm reached out. "Don't leave me!" he said weakly as he fell face forward and the yacht sped off.

"Oh you gonna make my friend very happy," Jainice said looking at Antonio unconscious body. Faith stepped out the house and looked up, most of the vans was off the block and everything was cleaned up, ten henchmen rushed pass her into Sabrina's house. She stopped one, "Collect all paperwork, computers and laptops and the nanny's, she come with us," Faith ordered.

"Yes Mistress," the henchmen said and ran into the house. Faith looked down at her son and kissed him on the forehead, "You're so cubby." she said and sat in the back of the Benz, staring into his eyes as her men cleaned everything up.

Lefty hopped into the driver seat then Jainice hopped in the seat next to Faith. "Told you it will all work out," Jainice said looking at the baby boy, "Oh God he looks just like Jason, I mean spitting image, you must have been mad as hell with him when you was pregnant." Jainice said.

"Not really I didn't get mad at him until the end of my pregnancy." Faith said.

"What's wrong, why you look like that?" Jainice asked noticing her facial expression.

"I don't know but something don't feel right, I still have that weird feeling in my stomach and Sabrina got away," Faith said looking out the window at Sabrina house.

"We found that bitch once and we will find her again Jainice said.

"Yea, after we get your brothers for killing Cricket," Lefty said cutting into the conversation.

"Lefty, I said we will get to that, don't stress it. What I'm saying is something about this situation don't feel right, I can't put my finger on it, something is off," Faith said.

"So you don't think that he's your son?" Jainice asked.

"No, he's my baby, I can feel the connection and he took his father's whole face. I'm just saying something wrong I don't know what it is." Faith replied.

"Well, I got a nice gift for you," Jainice said pointing ahead and Faith could see a henchmen loading up Antonio into the back of the van. "And he's still alive, I darted him for you," Jainice said smiling. Faith grinned.

"We got to get moving soon, the henchmen at the front gate said one cop car pulled in to check out the party and noise complaint." Lefty said and pulled off. Faith looked at Sabrina's house as they pulled off.

Chapter 9

The rain came down hard in Augusta Georgia. Faith held her son while looking out the window, she watched the rain then looked down at her son. She kissed him on the forehead, then walked to the kitchen and opened up the pantry door and pressed a button and it turned into an elevator and she rode it down to a secret compound base, about the size of half a block, Faith looked at the henchmen moving around minding their business then entered an all-white room. Jainice was sitting on a purple couch eating gummy bears, and looking at Antonio asleep strapped to a steel table and behind them was the pets in cages. Faith sat down next Jainice, "So how's my God-son?" Jainice asked and pass Faith three gummy bears.

"Are these like the worms?" Faith asking smiling.

"Naw, not as strong but still get you messed up, anyway how you like being a mother?" Jainice asked.

"The last week felt like heaven but I'm still a little off and don't know why, but I'm happy. Being a mother is great and having my son back is everything, I'll never take my eyes off him again." Faith responded.

"Good I don't like you stressed anyway. What you gonna name him? Jainice asked.

"His name is Damon." Faith replied and a henchmen walked in the room and handed her a bottle.

"Hmm I like it, it fits him, so you gonna keep the nanny or kill her?" Jainice asked.

"I swear when your high, you got a million questions?" Faith said smiling.

"But you know this bitch," Jainice said throwing a gummy bear at Jason's head and another one at Meashell. And watched them eat it.

"It should be a rule, no feeding no animal in the zoo." Faith said.

"Naw, I like when I get them high, I come in here and just think and feed them edibles. They be high as hell, geeked the fuck up, spinning in circles on all fours and shit," Jainice said eating more gummies.

"To answer your question, yea I'm gonna keep the nanny but have to break her first, which won't take long." Faith said as she turned around to see Lefty enter the room. We need to talk Lefty said and walk around the cough until he was in front of

Faith and Jainice. "What is it? Is everything running smoothly?" Faith asked.

"Yes, but that's not what we need to talk about, when are we going to get your brothers to revenge Cricket's death?" Lefty said with an attitude.

"Lefty, I don't like your tone, I told you already we will get to that, I just got my son back, it just been a week. I want to spend some time with him before I run out shooting shit up again." Faith said.

"So when, a week? A month? Two months? Cricket was one of us, family," Lefty said.

"Lefty, you're really blowing my high, I'm at peace. You need to stop asking me so many questions, your my friend but your crossing the line." Faith said.

"Give me an answer!" Lefty shouted.

Faith stood up with her son in her arms, "Listen you're taken my kindness for a weakness my friend. We will go after my brother when I fucking say so, and you better not ask me again. It could be a year or maybe two, it's what I say, you better act like you know." Faith said staring into Lefty eyes as he lowered his head as she sat back down.

Jainice looked with her eyes wide open and a smirk on her face from being high. Faith sat back down. "Don't make me speak to you like that again," Faith said while giving her son the bottle.

Lefty lifted up his head, "I thought you'd say that," Lefty said. Faith looked up to see Lefty pointing a dart gun at her and squeezed the trigger shooting her twice, once in the forehead and one in the chest, then he turned the gun to Jainice and shot her three times in the face.

"Lefty what you doing?" Faith said weakly as Lefty snatched Damon out her arms. "Lefty no," Faith was barely able to say as Lefty shot her again in the neck and she lost consciousness and slide off the couch on to the floor. "Ughhh!" Faith groaned while holding her head, "Fuck I got a killer headache," she said out loud then opened her to see she was on the floor. "Damon," she said then popped up off the floor she look around and didn't see him. Jainice was passed out on the couch and Antonio was still strapped to the table but the cages behind him with Jason, Regina and Meashell and the rest of her pets was now empty.

Faith ran out the room and the whole compound was quiet no henchmen around at all, she checked the other rooms and nothing. She then ran to the elevator and rode it up to the house, she ran to Damon's bedroom and he wasn't there. "What the fuck is going on?" Faith said while crying. "Jainice," Faith said then ran back to the elevator and road it down and dashed down the hallway back into the zoo room. She look at Jainice and grabbed her and started to shake her and lightly slapped her on the face but Jainice was knocked out cold.

"Mmm! Mmm!" Faith heard a mumbling sound and looked toward Antonio still strapped to the table, and a gag ball in his mouth, taped to his chest was a black iPad. Faith walked over to him and ripped the iPad off, and it started to ring. She look at it strangely then pressed answer. Lefty's face popped up for the video call. "Lefty what's going on, you darted me? Why would you do that? And where Damon?" Faith asked with an confuse look on her face.

"Damon is with me and you'll get him back if you listen," Lefty said.

"You took my child and now trying to black mail me, what the fuck is wrong with you Lefty? Stop this bullshit now!" Faith shouted not believing what she was hearing.

"This is no bullshit, you never really listen to me, like I told you, you have to show your face to more of the compounds and let the henchmen see you, but you didn't and let me run everything and assume responsibility, now I control over six of your compounds, the other six are still scared of you or think your father will pop back up but I think he's gone for good," Lefty said.

"What the fuck you took over the henchmen, why would you do that, you was only supposed to help me run things lighten the load for me as my friend," Faith said.

"And I was, but you never listened, so I did what's best for me Faith, now you will listen to me." Lefty replied.

"I can't believe this, you was like a brother to me, you know what I went through to get my son back, and you're doing this why, Lefty I love you." Faith said.

"Love isn't enough sometimes, I lost the one I loved, did you know Cricket was my husband? We married in Vegas and was gonna tell you but was scared to, my husband was so loyal to you and look where it got him. Killed. For what? For fucking what? You was playing with your brothers, you had six opportunities to kill them, all the henchmen seen it and told me, but you kept holding back until one of them got the drop on you and Cricket threw his life away. I'm mad at you and hurt you let his death mean little to nothing, then once you get your baby back, it was like fuck Cricket, I'm gonna live my happy life, fuck killing the ones that took his life because they're my brothers. Fuck that!" Lefty shouted.

"No it was never like that, I was going to revenge his death but I just got Damon back, I just wanted to spend time with him, to see what it felt like to be a mother," Faith said while crying.

"You can't have your joy until I have mine bitch," Lefty said and passed a henchmen the iPad as he stood back, he had Damon in his arms rocking him. Behind him Faith could see her pets, Doctors Rashi was led to the front by his leash on all fours. Six henchmen surrounding him and pulled out knives that started stabbing him repeatedly. Doctor Rashi made weird sounds as he tried to scream, and fell to the side and the henchmen continued to stab him until he stopped moving. Faith wiped the tears from her eyes and her whole demeanor changed, her heart went cold and dark. Lefty seen it and swallow the saliva in his mouth and got scared. He stuttered before he started to speak. "The longer you take to kill your brothers, we will kill one of your pets from the zoo, when you run out of pets we will kill Damon," Lefty said and started to get scared.

"Listen to me and listen to me clearly, you fuck up and any henchmen that follows you done fucked up. Lefty I'll make you into one of my pets for this and know I'm coming." Faith said and hung up the call.

Lefty and the henchmen looked at each other scared to death. "We know how she move, we will be okay." Lefty said trying to reinsure the henchmen but didn't really believe the words himself. "She gonna come for me, I think I broke her heart, she's gonna fucking chop me up. I got to think and try to outsmart her or we're all dead." Lefty said then looked down at Damon in his arms.

"Mmm! Mmm!" Antonio groaned through the gag ball trying to get Faith's attention. Faith dropped the iPad and looked at him with a look of death in her eyes. She looked on the far side wall and could see her double blade axe and grabbed it. "Mmmm mmm!" Antonio said as she now stood in front of him. Faith squinted her eyes then walked around him and unstrapped the gag ball, then stepped back around him and looked at him strapped to the steel table standing straight up.

Antonio licked his lips, "Wait, wait! I got information, can we make a deal?" Antonio said. Faith stood quiet then swung, chopping off his right leg under the knee cap. "Ahhhh!!!" Antonio screamed at the top of his lungs and looked down at the other half of his leg on the floor. "You got to be kidding!" Antonio screamed as Faith raised the axe to swing again. "Wait wait!" But his words went on death ears as she chopped of his left leg. "Uhhhh! Ahhh!" Antonio screamed in excruciating pain. "Please stop, no more no more!" Antonio pleaded. "Wait wait! I know where they're going with your baby and I got more information you don't know," Antonio said while crying. Faith stopped as she was about to swing again.

"Talk," Faith said in a nonchalant tone.

"Okay your men questioned me and asked how to find Sabrina they're going meet her in California. Sabrina will try to go somewhere cold, to hide." Antonio said and Faith was about to swing. "Wait there's more," Antonio said. Faith lower the double blade axe and could see a smile on his face, even with the pain he was in. "I was surprised you made it out that building alive after we shot you and cut you up. What really shock me is that you didn't know." Antonio said trying not to cry from the pain he was in.

"I didn't know what?" Faith asked.

"You didn't know about the second baby," Antonio said.

"The second baby," Faith said then touched her stomach.

"Yes the day we cut you open you, you passed out from the pain when we took Damon out of you but we noticed your stomach still moving, it was another sack, we took it out and it was a girl. We named her Hope. I'm surprise you didn't notice it or your men didn't say nothing about the second baby room. She looked just like you, dark-skin complexion with your big eyes. You let Sabrina run right pass you with her in her arms."

Faith's mind raced as Antonio talked, flashbacks of Sabrina's house played in her mind and how Sabrina ran down the stairs with something in her arms in a blanket and a briefcase. Faith dropped down to her knees. "The feeling I kept getting, when I kept telling myself something wasn't right, it was her calling me, and I just let her get snatched away again." Faith said to herself while crying.

Antonio started laughing while coughing. Faith look up at him. "I can't believe you didn't know," he said laughing even harder as Faith stopped crying and stood up. "Wait! Don't, I know how you can track my wife with bitcoins," Antonio said talking fast but wasn't fast enough Faith swung and the axe cut through half of his stomach, she pulled it out and swung again cutting off half his lower half then looked him in the eyes as he spit up chunks of blood. She then swung and the blade ate through the flesh of his neck and chopped his head completely off. His head flew across the room and hit the wall and bounced onto the floor. Jainice opened her eyes and sat up, while holding her head.

"Fuck I hate those darts," she groaned then looked up at Antonio mangled body. "What happened?" she said weakly.

"Get up we got to go?" Faith said.

"Go where?" Jainice asked.

"To kill a lot of people and get back my kids." Faith said.

"Kids, what the hell I miss? How long have I been a sleep shit?" Jainice said as she got up and seen Faith pick up Antonio's head and put it up under her arms like a football. "I guess he's not going into the zoo," Jainice said.

"Don't worry, I know two people who are," Faith said walking out the room and touched her stomach. "A girl." she mumbled to herself.

Coming Soon…

I Couldn't Hear Her Scream

Jasmine Davis sat up on her bed with her back resting against her headboard and two pillows as she held her Kindle Fire while reading intensely.

"Oh my God, baby you got to read this book Snapped by this author Shameek. He so sick in the fucking mind I swear but I love it." Jasmine stated. "Shhhh love I'm trying to sleep." Rick responded with his back turned to her and his covers pulled all the way up to his shoulders. He wiggled a little closer to her to be more comfortable.

Jasmine looked at him and sucked her teeth psst, twisted up her face and wanted to say something rude but held her tongue which is something she's been trying to work on when it comes to her husband. She fixed her bonnet on her head and straightened it out and went back to reading. "I don't know why you be reading those damn books by that author at night; you be paranoid as hell acting all scared and shit and thinking everyone after you for about three week straight and sleeping under me." Rick said while yawning.

"So what? That's the whole point of the book people believe shit can't happen to them but the book shows you it can and I believe it." Jasmine replied then reached under her pillows and touched the handle of her Glock 26 handgun. Just as a loud thumping noise could be heard. "Rick! Rick baby! Get up, get up! I heard a funny sound in the house just now." Jasmine said. "It's probably the girls sneaking down to the kitchen to get a snack or something and the ADT alarm didn't go off and the house still on lockdown, see." Rick said while pointing to the digital alarm panel on the wall next to the bedroom door. The light would turn green on the panel if any if the doors or windows would open, and a nonstop beeping would go off.

Jasmine looked at her bedroom door and a bubble feel hit her stomach and a chill went through her body. "Something isn't right baby, I'm telling you I can feel it. Rick just go check on the kids please, it will make me feel better." Jasmine said. "Ugh! Kids they're damn near grown, Traci sixteen and Melissa is eighteen, I'm pretty sure if something was wrong we would know by now." Rick said wishing she would just lay down and go to sleep so he can finally get some rest without her jumping every second from being scared. "I'm going take your kindle " she asked. "Nothing Baby." Rick replied. There was a loud thumping echo through the house again.

"See! See, Rick get up and check on it, aren't you the man of the house? Go check I'm not playing with you." Jasmine said while shaking his shoulders. "Ugh! Why didn't I marry a I'm nonparanoid woman that not into horror books and movies? I don't understand how you read and watch that shit just to be scared. I just wasn't some damn sleep." Rick said under his breath. "Well you got damn didn't! You married me and been happy for twenty seven years; so I must be doing something right, now get your big ass up and go check on our daughters. Now Rick!" Jasmine replied.

"Yea! Yea, yea." Rick said as he eased out their king size bed and grabbed his black robe off the floor that Jasmine had gotten him for Father's Day to slip it on, he rubbed his bald head. "God I wish I could back to sleep, she always scared of something." Rick thought to himself and headed toward the bedroom door. "Uhmm! Where you going?" Jasmine asked with a confused look on her face as if he'd lost his damn mind. Rick looked at her as if she were stupid and rolled his eyes." I'm going to check on the girls like you said dear." Rick replied in a sleepy tone. "Are you dump or stupid? Pick one." Jasmine replied.

"Huh what?" Rick said not really in the mood. "I really don't feel like doing this; God just let me go to bed." Rick thought to himself. "You're not dumb so you must be stupid. We just heard two loud ass thumping noise in our house and you about to walk out our bedroom and walk around our home with no weapon in your hand? Don't you watch the scary movies with me. You're asking to get snatched up by something, boy if you don't grab your gun out the nightstand before I kick you in the ass, because we're about to be fighting, you moving to damn slow." Jasmine said.

"Oh my God, I'm too old for this shit! You're too old for this shit! No more horror books, I can't take this right now. We have a full ADT alarm system that I pay for every fucking month; if a burglar or anything else got in, it would beep nonstop and the police would be here. My head hurt I'm sleeping on the couch tonight and don't dare bother me!" Rick shouted while going back to the bed and grabbing his pillow and a sheet off the bed and headed out the room.

"Wait baby, wait." Jasmine said but Rick was already down the hallway of their four bedroom house and headed down the stairs. "I didn't go too far, I know I didn't but I felt something weird in my bones, I'm not fucking crazy like he thinks I am." Jasmine thought to herself then heard another loud thumping sound echo throughout the house. She looked at the digital alarm panel and could see it was still on lock mode. "Fuck this shit! We should've gotten a dog like I said." she said out loud to herself and grabbed her small Glock 26 from under her pillows. She checked the clip making sure all ten bullets was in it then pulled back the chamber making a bullet pop in it. As soon as she did all the lights in the house went out.

"Oh hell no! Hell fucking no!" Jasmine said repeatedly as she got up from the bed and walked over to her bedroom window to look out of it, she looked up and down her block to see if the power was only out at her house but it wasn't, the whole block was experiencing the blackout. Jasmine exhaled with a sign of relief. Thank you God, Lord knows I was about to panic and lose my mind, she said out loud to herself as she put on her pink robe with the matching pink furry slippers and put her phone in her robe pocket but not before pressing 911 and all she had to do is press call. She grabbed her Kindle Fire and pressed a button on it. The screen was big and bright and the L.E.D light shined she held, using it as a flashlight while holding her Glock 26 in her other hand and slowly stepped out of her bedroom and walked down the hallway. Her heart was racing, pounding, and feeling as if it wanted to jump out of her chest.

"I should just calm down; my husband is right I always overreact." Jasmine mumbled to herself as she walked down the hallway of the second floor cautiously. The sound of weak groaning caught her attention, her facial expression twisted up and her left eyebrow raise, she made it to her daughter's bedroom and pushed it open and used her kindle for light and seen the bed was empty, she then checked the next bedroom to see that her other daughters' bed was empty as well. "Girls! Girls!" Jasmine called out in a whisper but got no response. She shut their room doors then turned around, they're bedroom was right next to the staircase, "Lord this is how shit starts , I know it, I feel it in my stomach."

"I should just call the police now." Jasmine said to herself while inching down the stairs slowly and using the Kindle Fire for light, she reached the first floor and flinched, jumping as if she was expecting something to jump out at her. "Rick baby! Traci! Melissa!" Jasmine called out in a whispered tone. She could hear a sound or weird noise in the living room. This would be the perfect time for the lights not to work she said to herself. The sound got louder as she got closer to the living room "Mhhmmmm!" She heard then seen a larger figure jump out at her. "Ahhhhh!" She screamed at the top of her lungs dropping her kindle and wasted no time to squeeze the trigger repeatedly to her Glock 26. The loud sound of the Glock echoed throughout the house as bright orange flames came out the gun. Seven bullets ricocheted through the large frame that ran toward her with full speed until it just stopped and stood stock in place then dropped to the floor.

"Got you motherfucker!" she said excited and nervous at the same time. Her hand was shaking uncontrollably as she picked up her Kindle Fire and walked closer to the body that was twitching and squirming on the floor. She used her Kindle Fire L.E.D light to shine at the floor. What she seen caused her to drop to her knees. "Noo! Lord Noooo Rick baby! Rick, baby get up! Baby get up! What have I done!" Jasmine screamed as blood gushed out of Ricks' body like a water bird. "Baby just hold on okay please hold on I'm going call the ambulance." Jasmine said in a panic and scared tone. "How can I be so stupid? How I didn't recognize your body shape? You warned me about being paranoid for years. Baby just hold on." Jasmine said while crying, tears steam down her cheeks, she used the back of hand to wipe them all, she dug in her pocket and grabbed her phone. "Oh God no! No!" she screamed as Ricks' body started shaking and went into convulsions and white foam came out his mouth then he stopped moving. "Baby! Baby no hold on." Jasmine said as she was about to press send on her phone, she felt a hard blow to the side of his head, hitting her in the temple and ear. She flew sideways onto the floor on to the blood soaking wooden floor. Jasmine tried to open her eyes but couldn't; it was as if they were glued shut, and a loud ringing sound could be heard only in her head and the taste of copper was in her mouth as if she were licking penny's like she did as a child. She spit out a mouth full of blood.

"What the fuck?" she mumbled as she felt as if she'd gotten hit by a truck. She moved her hand around to try and feel for the handle of her gun but felt nothing but another hard blow to her face. "Ahhh!" Jasmine screamed and then could feel pressure of something on her chest. "Yes bitch scream! I like when they scream." Jasmine could hear a man say but his voice sounded funny as if he was using one of those voice-box analyzers so people couldn't recognize your voice.

"Get off me! Get the fuck of me!" Jasmine screamed while trying to move her body but the man had to weigh a good hundred eighty pounds. He wasn't as big as her husband but still a big man. Jasmine head stopped hurting and she was able to finally open her eyes a little at a time. The throbbing in her temple eased just a little bit. She could see the man stepping on her chest. He had on a blue hoodie and with the lights off it was impossible to see his face. "God help me please!" Jasmine screamed while she continue to cry. "Yes! Yes scream for me bitch." the man in the hoodie said in a deep voice.

Jasmine facial expression twisted up in disgust and she fought back tears, knowing he was getting aroused from all of this, she lifted her head off of the floor and sure enough she could see his little dick trying to grow in his jeans. "You're enjoying this? You're fucking sick! You break into my home and harm my family just to get a turn on." Jasmine said while wiggling and fighting back tears. "Shut up!" screamed the man as he twisted around and jammed a knife into Jasmine stomach. "Ahhhhh!" Jasmine let out a piercing scream and her body bucked even harder trying with all her might to toss him off but it went in vain. "Yes! Yes, just like that, you and your daughters have beautiful voices, I can't explain it but it's one of a kind, it's like you passed down your high pitch voice to them. It sends sweet chills through my body, like eating some good ice cream too fast. You know should slow down and stop but you keep going even after the brain freeze." the hood man said with his hand still on the handle of the knife, he never pulled the knife out Jasmine's stomach after stabbing her with it. He looked at her face and noticed she had stop screaming once her body had gotten used to the pain.

"Fuck you! Fuck you, you bastard." she said while spit flew out her mouth. The hoodie man smiled then twisted the handle of the knife, the razor sharp blade twisted around in her insides, ripping tissue and flesh, feeling the hole. "I said scream!" the hoodie man said and was about to smile for the new scream Jasmine was about to let out. "Melissa, Jasmine's eighteen years old daughter stumbled into the room, blood was dripping out of the six stab wombs she has; her once cream night gown was now soak and the color of cranberry. She held her chest with her right hand trying to slow down the blood from pumping out of what use to be her breast, in her left hand she gripped a butcher knife. "Get off my mother!" she screamed weakly and stabbed the hoodie man in the rib with all her might while using her body weight to push it in deeper. "Ugggh! Ahh! You bitch!" he groaned in agonizing pain as he fail sideways on the blood soaked floor.

"Yea you scream bitch. How it feel?" Jasmine screamed. "Baby kill him! Get the gun!" Jasmine shouted weakly while trying to get off the floor and stand up but she stumbled a few times before getting her balance. Her head was still spinning and the water in her eyes made it hard to see from the tears she was fighting back. "Baby get the gun, mommy can't see, it's too dark." Jasmine said to her daughter but didn't hear no response or see her moving. Melissa was laid out in the floor on her stomach. "Baby get up, don't close your eyes, don't quit, we're not quitters." Jasmine said and scanned the floor her Glock 26. She spotted it up under the dining room table. "Momma I can't move, hurry momma get him." Melissa said while coughing up blood. Melissa and Jasmine looked over at the man in the hoodie and could see him tossing around on the floor, rolling side to side while holding his ribs. He was good at giving out pain but terrible at receiving the shit. The long kitchen knife was still jammed into his left side in his rib cage; he acted as if he was scared to pull it out.

"I'm going fucking kill you." he groaned as Jasmine looked back at him while she limped toward the dining room table. When she finally reached it, she squatted down to reach the gun next to the chair leg. The man in the hoodie knew what she was doing and worked up the nerves he needed and pulled out the knife from his side and held his wound. He hopped to his feet as fast as he could just as Jasmine touched the handle of the gun with the tip off her fingers. The man with the hoodie ran and jump in the air and came down with all his strength. "Ahhhhh!" Jasmine hollered as the razor sharp knife came down and cut off four of her fingers at once. "Aughhh! Ahhh!" she screamed in excruciating pain. Blood pump out where her fingers use to be, she put her hand to her face and tried to wiggle her fingers as she couldn't believe that her fingers weren't really there. She only had her thumb left.

The man with the hoodie bent down and picked up the gun and tucked the knife in his waist band behind his belt. He aimed the gun at Jasmine, who was now pressing her fingers against her chest to slow down the bleeding. "I really don't like using guns but you bitches are something else, this supposed to be fun, but since I been in this house I been knocked over the head with something twice and stabbed, this is way too much." the man with the hoodie said while coughing. "That just means your soft and go after people you can walk over, but you're going cross the wrong family and get your ass really hurt, this isn't a game. I taught my girls to never give up, when they play sports, run track or baseball; I tell them to keep going, keep fighting until the last breath and that's what you going get out of us; us fighting and keep going until the last breath, you going regret stepping foot in this home. I promise you that." Jasmine said with snot dripping down her nose while she cried. Her body was consumed by pain; it was a part on her that didn't hurt. It was a miracle she hadn't pass out yet. But then adrenaline mixed with anger and concern for her family kept her going.

Jasmine could see her daughter Melissa in the living room somehow still breathing and looking at her while on the floor. She had another kitchen knife in her hand, this one was smaller than the one before. "Where the hell she hide that one, never mind." Jasmine thought to herself. "I really wanted to hear you scream some more but I'm running out of time." the man with the hoodie said as he leveled the gun with the center of Jasmine forehead. He let out light chuckles as he began to squeeze the trigger. He heard a weak voice scream, "To our last breath," then felt a sharp blade rip through the flesh and muscle of his back calf muscle. "Ahhh!" he hollered Melissa grabbed his leg and pulled the knife out; she was still on her stomach from being too weak to stand. She grabbed his jeans and used them to help pull herself up off the floor. The man with the hoodie couldn't believe his eyes, she was soaked with her own blood and lost count how many times he had stabbed her, last time she was bleeding out in a puddle of blood.

Melissa had gotten fully up and jumped on to his back. The hoodie man tried to buck and shake her off. Melissa looked at her mother. "Now momma!" she shouted. "You crazy bitches, what's wrong with y'all?" as Jasmine grabbed his right hand with her left hand and tried to get the gun. "You crazy ass hoes; the whole fucking family crazy." the man with the hoodie shouted and was about to curse again but Jasmine got up and stuffed her hand that had no fingers into his mouth. "Watch your mouth in my damn house." Jasmine shouted while stuffing her hand more into his mouth. The man in the hoodie couldn't believe what was happening and before he could react he felt a sharp pain repeatedly in his back as Melissa stab him over and over with the little knife. "Ahhhh!" he tried to scream but it was muffled by Jasmine hand in his mouth. He yanked his hand free of Jasmine's grip and squeezed the trigger to the gun, sending a bullet ripping through the meat of her thick thigh. Jasmine backpedaled as the heartburn sensation in her leg was too much to bare and she fell straight to the floor once again. Once he noticed Jasmine was down he wasted not wasting time and bucked his body and flip Melissa over his shoulders off his back and she landed next to her mother.

Melissa turned and looked at her mother with tears in her eyes and mumble something just as her head split open into two , her brains and tissue and bones flew everywhere as the man with the hoodie stood over her with the smoking gun. "Noooo! Noo not my baby!" Jasmine screamed as she stared at what use to be her daughter and touched her chin and lips gently. The hoodie man raise the gun again and aim at the back of Jasmine head. Traci was passed out on the floor in the kitchen next to the refrigerator. She open her eyes and look around as her head throbbed. "What happened?" she said to herself then remember coming down stairs to the kitchen to get something to eat then the power went out and someone hit her on the back of the head. She went to reach and touch her head but she quickly realized her hands was zip tied behind her back.

She tried to pull them apart and break them but couldn't the sound of her mother and sister screaming and sound as if they were fighting made her heart skip a beat. She sat up on her butt and scooted closer to the refrigerator and rest her back against it and use it to help her stand up. She walked backward to a drawer and pull it open and grabbed a knife and cut the zip tie until her hands was free. The sound of a gunshot stopped her in her tracks as everything went silent. "No." she said to herself.

Jasmine body trembled with fear and anger, "How my whole family die from a fucking sick killer? This must be a terrible joke." Jasmine thought to herself as she felt like giving up and knew it was over, she lowered her head and kissed her daughter chin then turned around and faced the man in the hoodie as he pointed the gun at the center of her head, just like he did Melissa. "God forgive me for all my sins and thank you for the life you gave us." Jasmine prayed as she waited for death. "Ahhhhh! Get away from my mother dick head!" Jasmine heard her youngest daughter scream just as the man in the hoodie was about to squeeze the trigger.

"Traci stabbed him in the head with the knife she took from the kitchen, the bullet flew out the gun missing Jasmine. "Fuck! Fuck? Ahhhh! It can't be this difficult to kill y'all bitches." the man in the hoodie shouted as he turn around and punch Traci in the nose sending her flying backwards into the air and causing her to lose consciousness. "What the fuck is wrong with you people, normal people don't act like this, they get scared then barely fight and accept the fact they're going get killed, you people are fucking insane. I been getting my ass beat all fucking night long." he said while trying to pull the knife out his head but it was in there to deep. "Straight bullshit I thought I was the serial killer. these bitches are something else, some wild fucking animals. I'm just ready to get out of here, they took all the joy out the screams for me tonight." the man with the hoodie said to himself then kicked Jasmine in the chin. "Fuck the women in this family. I killed the damn father easy, Fuck this I swear." he said as he finally pulled the knife out his hand and turn around and grabbed Traci by her leg and drag her body to the front door.

"I'm going take your little psychopath and make her pay for what you and your other daughter did to me for ruining my damn night. I had two more homes to do after this; I can't go bleeding all over the place." the man with the hoodie said as he dragged Traci out the house into the cold winter night of Detroit. Snow had just started to fall as he stuffed Traci's unconscious body into the trunk of his car. "Noo! Noo, not my baby! Not my baby!" Jasmine cried out as she opened her eyes and fought the pain, thinking of her daughter and forgetting the pain she was in and crawled to the front door. The man with the hoodie smiled as he looked at Jasmine hanging half way out her front door on the floor with her arm stretched out as if she were trying to reach him. "Don't take my baby! Noo!" Jasmine screamed while crying hysterically. The man with the hoodie hopped into his car and pulled off disappearing down the dark streets.

I Couldn't Hear Her Scream

NATIONAL BESTSELLING AUTHOR
SHAMEEK A. SPEIGHT
AUTOR OF A CHILD OF A CRACKHEAD SERIES

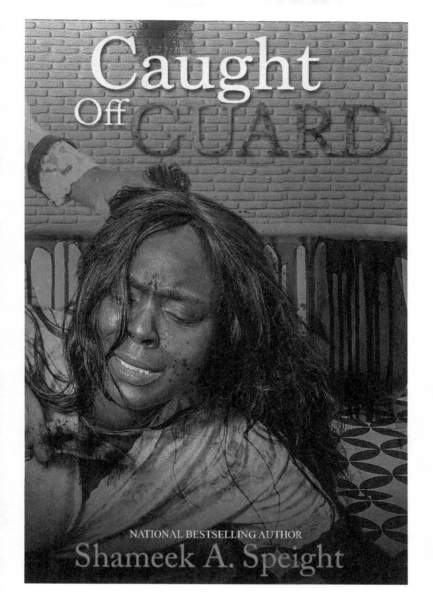

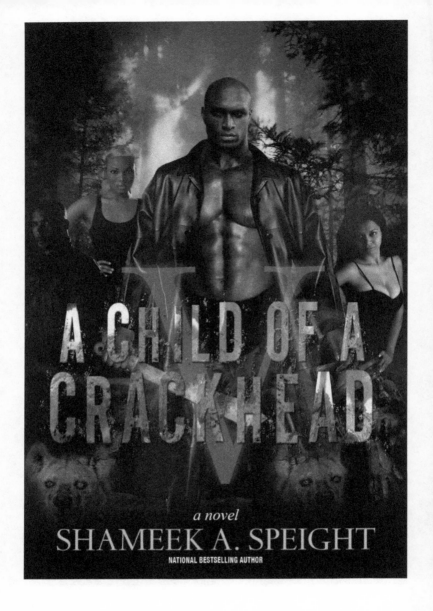

A CHILD OF A CRACKHEAD

a novel

SHAMEEK A. SPEIGHT

NATIONAL BESTSELLING AUTHOR

Join my Mailing List by texting
shameekspeight to
844-484-0922

CPSIA information can be obtained
at www.ICGtesting.com
Printed in the USA
LVHW111653140822
725922LV00002B/181